THE WOMAN I WANT DEAD

A sequel to 'The Woman I Befriended'

By Sara Kate

Cover Design by Methodical Video Productions.
ISBN Ebook: 978-1-7358325-8-6
ISBN Paperback: 978-1-7358325-9-3
First Edition: May 2024

This book is dedicated to my husband and father who are always my first readers, anyone who enjoys reading my work and anyone who encourages me to keep writing.

THE WOMAN I WANT DEAD

AVERY, FL

TIFFANY

October 8th

Sirens roar. Red and blue lights flash in the distance ahead of me as I see a cop car turn left down my street.

Shit. Another police car is speeding up behind me. I pull over, hoping my fate isn't about to end, but he speeds by me. It's time to turn around and get out of this town immediately. This is all thanks to Ellie and her sidekick, Chloe. What a shame, because I actually considered Chloe as a friend to me until she introduced me to Ellie.

It was a poor decision of mine to leave that man alone in my attic this morning, but what else was I supposed to do? When those bitches started following me back home, it was too late. My only option was to kill all three of them, except I was only prepared to kill *him.*

While heading back down the road, the opposite

way of my house—or should I say, *my old house*, three more patrol cars speed by me.

Once things settle around here, I will come back to Avery and make those bitches pay for what they are about to make me do.

TIFFANY

A year & 3 months later

The headlights from Chloe's Jeep illuminate the curtain outside of her living room window. I get up from the couch where I have been patiently waiting for her to return home from work.

I rush down the hallway to hide in her bathroom, closing the door behind me.

Because of Ellie and her curious mind, Chloe will have to bear the brunt of the consequences to her actions tonight. Ellie will endure her fate later on.

The thud of the front door shutting is faint, followed by footsteps in the hallway a few minutes later.

The bathroom door creaks open as I remain hiding in the sneakiest, yet the most obvious spot available—behind the shower curtain. After I hear Chloe use the bathroom, the sound of the faucet runs and I hold my breath in anticipation, praying that she will opt for a shower after a long night of working at the bar rather than go straight to bed.

When the faucet stops running, my hope is quickly fulfilled as the shower curtain slides over. A wide-eyed Chloe appears on the other side.

"Surprise." I smile. A quick scream escapes her lungs before I tackle her to the floor. She lands on her back. I bang her head repeatedly against the tile. Over, over, and over again.

Then I slash the side of her head one time, leaving a pool of blood underneath her body.

Rest in peace, Chloe Jones.

FAIRVIEW, FL

2 Years Later

ELLIE

1

When a serial killer is pursuing you, the only way to live without being in utter fear is to be prepared for when she finds you. That's why I have taken the precaution of installing an alarm system and security cameras inside of my house and around my entire property.

While waiting for my new client to arrive, I open the blinds on my window to let some natural light into my home office. What used to be my view of several houses in a small neighborhood is now replaced with dense woods which surrounds my property. My new house now sits at the end of a dirt road that separates the greenery from my new front yard.

Two years ago, I lived an hour away from here in a small-town called Avery where houses surrounded me. Here in this rural town of Fairview, which is even smaller in population, I have to drive a mile down my dirt road, then another mile down the main road to get to my nearest neighbor.

Moving an hour away from where I unmasked *Tiffany Burnes* — the nation's most wanted and prolific serial killer, sounds like a poor choice of mine, but moving the short distance was the only option.

When Tiffany last contacted me years ago, she admitted to knowing my husband, Noah's travel schedule for work, so he demoted himself from full-time marketing director to part-time. He went from spending his days in an office and hopping planes a few months out of the year to conducting zoom meetings in our backyard. One of the spare bedrooms is designated as his office, but he uses it more for storing files and his books instead. The only positive thing that has come out of our uprooted lives is seeing more of my husband at home and his uplifted mood now that he is out of an office and gets to work outside.

But although he works from home now, he has to drive into Avery for meetings every few months, which is what really came down to our decision in moving to Fairview. Traveling anywhere outside of an hour for work seemed too risky when it comes to his safety. Public transportation is no longer safe as long as Tiffany remains on the run, but driving in our own vehicles is.

You would think moving to a secluded area in the woods as opposed to living in a populated neighborhood is dangerous since a serial killer is targeting me, but that's not exactly the case for my situation. Living out here makes it easier for me to notice when somebody is lurking around my home. With no neighbors in the vicinity, the only people who should ever drive down my dirt road apart from myself, are my husband and my clients. Not even the mailman because my mailbox is located at the end of road at the entrance.

When you live around people, it becomes easy for a person to commit a crime in the neighborhood without being noticed. As long as a person knows the neighbor's routines, it isn't that difficult to commit a crime. I can attest to this from my own experience. When I lived in Avery, I walked into the backyard of my neighbor, Chloe's house during broad daylight without anyone batting an eye.

That same neighbor also died only fifty feet away from me while I was across the street eating breakfast with my husband. We had no idea she was being murdered until Tiffany texted me about her heinous crime. See what I mean about not being noticed? As long as you observe your surroundings carefully, the rest comes easy.

Although I can't enjoy observing the neighbors here in Fairview like I used to do in Avery, I have learned to enjoy the quaintness of living in a house on an acre of land. Even though this house is about forty years older than our last one, which causes the structure to creak loudly and keep me awake at night, I *do* enjoy living here. I just hate that it wasn't my choice to move to this town on my own terms. I want to enjoy this place because *I chose* to enjoy it — not because I had to make a decision to move out of my hometown only to feel somewhat safer.

If Avery's police department caught Tiffany Burnes when I broke into her house with Chloe, my husband and I wouldn't have had to uproot our lives from what we were used to for almost a decade. If our lives hadn't changed, I would be drinking wine for most of my day while watching the routines of my neighbor's and taking collection payments over the phone. Noah does not miss going to the office every day and I don't miss my old collections job.

I only miss the thrill of observing the neighborhood from my window every day. And yes, my admiration for people watching became a bit too much of a perilous hobby. Admittedly, dangerously too much — So much that my curiosity and obsession of people watching landed me in the attic of a serial killer's home, and the reason for a friend dying.

Now here I am, nearly sheltered out in these woods until I catch her.

2

January 7th
12:00 p.m.

An alert on my computer distracts me from gazing out of my office window at the woods.

There are five security cameras that are set up on the outside of my house. The live feed from each camera is in a grid on my computer. Through the camera that is mounted on my front porch, I see a black pickup truck parked in my driveway.

The view from my office window overlooks the side of my house where the backyard is cornered up to the woods. My front yard and the direction of where vehicles come in from on the dirt road are not in my view from here, so I didn't see the truck pull in.

Standing about six-foot one in a blue button-down T-shirt, my client, Ben rings my doorbell.

Ben contacted me through my website yesterday morning regarding his brother, Cameron who disappeared two days ago. Ben said he tried to file a missing person's report at the police department here in Fairview, but the department didn't adhere. Therefore,

Ben decided to contact me which is usual in situations like his. When a person is looking for a family member or a friend and has exhausted all efforts with law enforcement, their next and only option is to seek out a private investigator if it fits in their finances.

Two months after Chloe died, I quit my collections job and decided to become a P.I. After completing two years of schooling, I added my name to the list of five investigators here in Fairview only three months ago. Shockingly for a small town, and more than one investigator in the area, Ben is about to become my fourth client in this business altogether.

After greeting him at the front door, I lead him down the hallway past the bedroom and Noah's office, then into mine.

Once we are acquainted, he takes a seat in the chair in front of my desk. I begin by asking him to tell me about the last time he saw his brother. "So how can I help you?"

"Well, given what I read on your website, I thought you would be very capable in helping me out." Ben shifts in his seat. "I reported Cameron missing to the police yesterday at around one o'clock in the afternoon once I realized that he wasn't coming home. He told me he was going on a date the night before with a woman who he met off a dating app. They had plans to meet for dinner at Angelinos restaurant. I figured he slept over her place after their date but when he didn't come home yesterday morning to change into his work clothes, I called and texted him a bunch of times. He never answered."

"And you mentioned in your email, the police

didn't list him in the system as missing," I say while searching for Cameron Robinson in the missing persons database for the town of Fairview.

No results found.

Ben shakes his head. "The police believe he skipped town, but that's not true."

"Why do the police think that?"

"Well, my brother has a history of drug abuse. He was addicted to cocaine for about two years." Sighing, Ben straightens up. "He's been sober for the past year and two months though. The police asked me if he had any history of drug or alcohol abuse. I said yes because he did, but I wish I hadn't because as soon as I said that, they immediately dismissed me. I think they believe Cameron relapsed, so that's why they didn't list him as missing. But I'm positive, that is not what happened. Cameron didn't relapse. I was just being honest with the police about his history. I shouldn't have though."

"Sometimes honesty bites you in the ass." I sigh.

"You ain't lying." Ben huffs. "When the police didn't help me, I contacted every P.I. in town. You were the first one to answer my email yesterday."

That makes sense because I'm the newest investigator in Fairview who isn't working an active case right now. I can guarantee my competition is working on more than one case at a time, even in this small town.

"What does your brother do for work?" I ask Ben.

"He's a handyman. He works for a small company that sends him on odd jobs like painting houses, cleaning pools, installing carpet. Anything really."

I summarize all the information that I have gained from our conversation so far, and type it into a note on my computer. "Okay, let me get the timeline of his disappearance straight. You said Cameron had plans to meet his date two nights ago which was the fifth at Angelinos. Do you know what time they were supposed to meet there?"

"Eight thirty. He left at eight o'clock."

"You said, Cameron met this woman off a dating app? Do you know if that was the first time they were meeting in person?"

Ben nods. "That's what he told me."

While typing, I ask. "Did he drive his own vehicle to meet his date or call a ride?"

"He drove his truck there. It's a black Ford F-150. I believe the year of the truck is 2009 or 2010. Not that it really matters anyways because I tried reporting his truck missing to the insurance company after I left the police station. I drove to Angelinos because I wanted to see if his truck was in the parking lot but it wasn't. Apparently, since I'm not on his policy, the insurance company couldn't help me either."

I am astonished at how much Ben has already done on his own and also quite relieved because his actions have made my job just a bit easier. Now hopefully, he can answer my next two questions. "Do you know the name of Cameron's date and the dating app he was using?"

"He didn't tell me her name, but he might've told me the name of the app. I can't remember though."

He looks down toward his feet, sighing. "I feel like a shitty brother right now."

"Don't be so hard on yourself. You've already done quite a lot."

If only Ben knew that I can relate to the guilt he's feeling. Because of what he read on my website, he knows about my involvement in the Tiffany Burne's case. What he doesn't know is that I am responsible for her first female victim and the reason as to why she's now on the run.

"Did Cameron happen to show you a photo of the woman he had plans to meet?" I ask Ben.

Again, he shamefully shakes his head.

"Alright. I'm going to need yours and Cameron's address, his date of birth, his social media handles, and any other pertinent information that you can think of. I'm going to email you a questionnaire right now. Fill it out to the best of your ability and write down anything else that you feel would be helpful in finding him. Once the retainer fee is paid, I'll start working on his case right away."

"Thank you!" Ben's shoulders drop, his body relaxing in his seat. "Thank you so much." He stands up to shake my hand.

Nodding, I return the handshake. "You're very welcome. But I want you to understand that I can only promise to do my best to find out what happened to your brother. Even though, my goal is to find him safely, unfortunately, I cannot promise you that I will. I just want you to be prepared for whatever the outcome might be."

"That's completely understandable. The reason I contacted you is because of your history with Tiffany

Burnes. What really impressed me when I read about you on your website, is that you were the one to bring her to the attention of the police. Because of that, I am confident you can help me figure out what happened to my brother. This is a pretty small-town. I can't imagine what could have happened to him here but then again, nobody imagined a serial killer could come out of Avery either." He shakes his head.

At least Ben knows what I am capable and not capable of. Well, slightly. He is aware that I built an investigation around Tiffany from what I wrote on my website. He just doesn't know about the obstacles I encountered, along with the danger I put myself and the people around me in during that time.

I brought a serial killer to the attention of the police and saved a man from being murdered. However, my efforts have not led me to figuring out where the hell that killer has been hiding out since then.

You would think breaking into a psychopathic woman's home, saving a man from fallen victim in her attic, and exposing a burial site that contained eight of her victims would satisfy me, but not even close. I will be truly satisfied when the woman is dead.

After Ben leaves my office, I watch him reverse his truck out of my driveway through the camera feed on my computer. Years ago, it was difficult for me to understand why my previous therapist chose to see patients in her home office. At the time, it seemed dangerous to allow random strangers into her household. Now I laugh at the irony as I just did the same thing for the fourth time since becoming a P.I.

Inviting patients into my therapist's house

baffled me before, but now I understand the logic. This is the place where I am most protected; here in my own home. Nobody knows this house like I do, so I should always feel safe—even when inviting a stranger in.

And I do feel safe. Although I am not thrilled about what led me to moving here, I have still made an effort to make this house my sanctuary and a place where nobody can outsmart or harm me, especially Tiffany.

After all, when you've become the target of a serial killer, you need to have all the protection you can get: An alarm system, security cameras that cover the outside and inside of your property, connections with law enforcement, and a legal weapon for self-defense.

I have all four.

3

January 7th
1:30 p.m.

Ready to mentally torture myself, I roll my corkboard of notes regarding details on the Tiffany Burnes investigation, out of the closet in my office.

Shame, guilt, anger, sadness, and fear runs through me each time my eyes lock onto her picture; the only recent photo that can be found of the psychopath, courtesy of me. Had I known my very amateur photography skills would be seen across the nation, I would have chosen a better spot at the go-go bar to capture a clearer photo of her while she was working that night. Only a small, *very small,* piece of closure sits somewhere deep inside of me when I remind myself that if it weren't for my reckless actions years ago, several deceased men would still remain lost in a missing persons database.

Even though I was clever and brave enough to build a case around Chloe who I befriended out of false intentions before shifting my investigation to the real killer, I am not satisfied and most definitely not happy with myself either.

When I think back to the months that I spent fixating all of my attention on Chloe from my window, then mistakenly deemed her Avery's serial killer, the guilt becomes unbearable. Even when I confronted her with my evidence and she revealed her past, I still didn't believe her. I treated her like a suspect when the whole time, I should have been treating her like a true friend. After weeks of shifting my investigation away from Chloe, my accusations led me to Tiffany, along with a strange friendship that developed between Chloe and I. A friendship which ended up being short lived *because* of Tiffany.

How my theory led me to the real killer was merely an unfortunate small-town coincidence and a consequence of my own actions — Actions that will probably haunt me for the rest of my life. And with tomorrow being two years since Tiffany murdered Chloe, both women have been heavily on my mind lately.

My attention shifts over to the information under the words 'WHAT I KNOW' pinned on the right side of the investigation board next to Tiffany's photo.

- TECHNIQUE OF MURDER: Drugs her victims, bludgeons them with an unknown heart shaped weapon, cuts bodies up with an axe
- Currently 24 years old
- Height: 5'8. Tan to dark skin, slim body Changes her appearance through makeup, wigs, outfits, and speaks different dialects

- TARGETED VICTIMS: men in their mid-twenties to early thirties
- KNOWN VICTIMS: 8 males and 1 female
- FAMILY: Adoptive mother (Billie) Older sister (Dianne) (both never suspects in investigation)

On the left side of my board, there is a list of unanswered questions.

- Where did she go after coming back to Avery to kill Chloe?
- Where was she during the few months before then?
- Where is she currently?
- What drives her to kill/motive?

Two more questions remain in the back of my mind and not on the board: *What is her next move with me? And when does she plan to make it?*

My eyes drift over to the thread of messages Tiffany sent me the night she killed Chloe. After confessing to her murder and proclaiming she caught on to our suspicions of her before then, she ended her lengthy text with a promise to me.

Ellie, you and I will reconnect soon. Until then, I'll be keeping tabs on you.

I haven't heard from her since then.

A knock on my door startles me for only a moment even though I know it is my husband on the other side. Three years ago, I would have hurried to hide my investigation board back in the closet upon hearing his presence, but things have changed since then. After he found me in a police station with Chloe, I made a promise to the both of us: *no more secrets from my husband, no matter how out of pocket my theories may be.*

"Come in," I call out. "My client just left a few minutes ago."

"How'd the meeting go?" Noah asks when opening the door. He walks in and sits in the chair that is meant for my clients. "I can't wait to get this thing off me." He sighs, grabbing a pen out of the cupholder on my desk and sticks it down the cast on his right arm. "These things really do get itchy."

A few days ago, Noah decided to take down the Christmas lights on our roof when I was out grocery shopping. He slipped when he was climbing halfway down the ladder, and broke his arm when he landed on it. We are both equally desperate for the cast to come off which isn't for at least another two to three weeks.

"The meeting went well. I'm just waiting for him to pay the retainer fee now. His brother, Cameron is missing. He tried reporting him to the police but they won't put him in the database because of Cameron's history with drug abuse. My client believes the police think he relapsed except he swears his brothers still sober. I need to find out what the police say about this myself, but his disappearance does feel off to me. Ben genuinely seemed concerned about his brother and the situation of Cameron's disappearance *is* a little peculiar."

"Always go with your instincts." Noah reminds me. "We know you've proved us all wrong before."

Smiling at his comment, I laugh because we both know he is right. My instincts brought attention to Tiffany Burnes. I just wish my instincts could figure out where she went after all that attention was brought onto her. My eyes drift over to the text messages on my board again.

I knew you and Chloe were on to me when you started coming to the bar more often than usual. I saw the tension at first, how you both looked at me and kept whispering like little gossip girls.

Regrettably, Tiffany's text message confirmed that Chloe and I weren't acting as secretive as we thought during the time of our amateur sleuthing. I do recall having a slight doubt about my discreetness when Tiffany stopped to hug me the night I went to follow one of her customers out of the bar. I had a suspicion she caught on to what I was doing and as it turns out, I was right which is why I believe strongly in my instincts.

And my instincts are telling me there is something off about Cameron's disappearance. I hope he isn't in danger except my gut tells me otherwise.

"What are you thinking?" Noah sits back, smirking. "I can tell your mind is already running."

I divert my attention from the board to my husband. "Well, my client said his brother had plans to meet a woman from some dating app for dinner the night he went missing."

"That's strange." Noah remarks, intrigued.

"What do you think could have happened?"

"I'm not too sure yet. Besides running a background check on him, I need to find out if he made it to the restaurant first. I also need to talk to the police to hear from them myself. Ben said they wouldn't list Cameron as missing because of his past, but maybe there's more to it."

If Cameron made it to Angelinos and met his date, I need to find out who she is. Ben did not have the slightest clue of what the dating app is called or the name of Cameron's date which means finding the woman is going to be a stretch. Although, this is nothing that I can't and haven't handled already.

Before becoming a private investigator, my first unofficial investigation as an unqualified citizen led me to the discovery of Tiffany Burnes. If I could handle that before even obtaining a proper investigative license, then I can take on whatever Cameron's case entails.

"How are you feeling by the way?" Noah asks.

"I'm alright, just frustrated." I sigh, reverting my eyesight back to Tiffany's photo. "I'm just mad that she's still on the run. I do think it's a good thing that Ben contacted me though. Working on a case is probably a good distraction for me right now. It's not like I'm swamped with other cases anyways. I just started working in this business and I'm already on my fourth client in a span of three months. I think that's a good thing, right?"

Noah nods. "That's a great thing. I'm really proud of you."

"I know." I smirk. "I'm going to visit Chloe tomorrow morning before I look into the case. That is, if

Ben pays the retainer fee by then, which I'm pretty sure he will because he was already very adamant about finding his brother."

"I would be too if I had a sibling," Noah says.

"I guess I would too." I agree, shrugging because both Noah and I are only children in our families. "I can't imagine what he's feeling."

Growing up without any siblings was one of the many similarities that we bonded over when we first started dating.

"What about you? How are you feeling about everything lately?" I ask him.

"I'm fine. I just want to make sure you're doing okay. I would love to go with you to the cemetery tomorrow, but I need the wi-fi for my meeting in the morning. Unless you want to wait for the meeting to end, then I can go with you."

"Don't worry about it."

My supportive saint of a husband deserves a reward for dealing with what I put him through when we lived in Avery. For months, I lied to him about my whereabouts and who I was befriending. Noah was only looking out for my mental sanity and safety, yet those two things were not my biggest concern back then. To say Tiffany put a strain on our relationship for a brief moment of time is an understatement.

However, allowing my mind to wander back to the past right now, regardless of tomorrow being the two-year anniversary of Chloe's death, will do no good for me. Tomorrow is just another day. Another day to get through.

Ding. An alarm on my phone reminds me it's

two o'clock in the evening.

Speaking of not letting my mind wander, it's time to leave for my group therapy session.

4

January 7th
2:30 p.m.

To my surprise, group therapy has been a slightly better experience for me than individual therapy has. Listening to other people share their feelings allows me a chance to stay silent instead of being asked to talk about my problems during the entire session. A lot of the times, I even get away with skipping my turn. In individual therapy, the spotlight remained on me the entire hour and I never liked being in the spotlight.

Listening to other people speak about their grief also comes with enduring the stories of hearing other people's trauma. Their stories regarding their experiences with death brings me to realize that I'm not alone in what I've endured, but it also causes thoughts of my own personal trauma that I have no desire to think about. Such as thoughts of my childhood best friend, Laura who has been dead for five years and then Chloe, the first and only friend of mine after that, whose been dead for two.

But just because there are opportune moments to

remain silent in this group, I can't *always* choose to skip my turn, like right now. Along with six other grievers, our psychologist Dr. Bennett, is staring at me. Everyone is waiting for me to share and this is why I don't like being in the spotlight. It's uncomfortable. I could choose to keep what is really on my mind a secret, but I have skipped my turn during the last two sessions and I don't know what else to come up with. Might as well tell the truth. And when I say truth, I mean, my version of the truth.

"Tomorrow makes two years since Jamie died," I say. Sighs and headshakes fill the ambience of the room. "I plan to visit her at the cemetery tomorrow," I tell the group, thinking about the hour drive from Fairview to Avery.

"I think going to see Jamie will bring you some peace with her passing," Dr. Bennett says.

Or it might cause insomnia for the next two weeks.

During my first therapy session with this group, I replaced Chloe's name with 'Jamie' because I can't tell the truth about why I started coming here. Nobody here needs to know that I am the reason for my friend's murder.

When Chloe's death made the news as Tiffany's ninth victim, the story immediately caused the public to speculate on why Chloe was suddenly specifically targeted. Especially since the public just learned about Tiffany as a killer who specifically targeted males only a few months before that. Nobody understands what the connection between the two women were.

Detective Carner, my husband, Chloe, my

previous therapist, and Jake (the man who I rescued from dying in Tiffany's attic with Chloe) are the only people who know that the connection is me.

In order to talk about what I went through without anyone in this group making a connection to Tiffany Burnes, I decided to tell a different version: *Jamie was a neighbor and a friend of mine who was murdered in her own home while I was sleeping across the street from her. It was a burglary gone wrong; a tragic mishap.*

Not as tragic as they think. For my safety, Detective Carner who works lead on the investigation requested that I keep my involvement out of the public until Tiffany is caught. If I did not go on to pursue a career as a private investigator, I would have listened, but with no cases under my belt, I had to start somewhere.

While keeping the story as brief as possible, I wrote about how my amateur sleuthing led me to Tiffany Burnes and the decision to becoming a Private Investigator:

During months of investigating a handful of disappearances in Avery's local missing persons on my own, I focused specifically on a group of males who all shared similarities in their disappearances. I, then, brought my evidence as a mere civilian to the police department who graciously reviewed everything in a timely manner. I successfully gained support of the local police in the investigation, bringing justice to several families and sparking an investigation into a beloved towns tragedy.

From what Ben said in our meeting; the words I

chose clearly worked to my avail. Imagine if I included the truth about what really led me to Tiffany?

After watching my neighbor Chloe, obsessively for months, I befriended her, then deemed her Avery's serial killer. I broke into her house, threatened her with an umbrella, then accused her of murdering several men. Then when she was forced to tell me about her traumatic past and proved she wasn't the killer, I later shifted my investigation to her coworker, Tiffany Burnes.

Chloe and I followed Tiffany home from work one morning, then broke into her house and rescued a man. Then I presented my evidence to the police, and now I am responsible for Tiffany being on the run and the reason as to why Chloe fell victim to her heinous crimes. A person died because of me and the killer isn't caught, but you should still call me to find your missing loved one.

A statement like that wouldn't gain me any clients at all. Yes, my actions were a little impulsive and not thoroughly thought out back then, but don't let the past determine the present.

After all, my sudden relentless theories and actions were the reason why I shifted careers into private investigation. Clearly, my inquisitive personality has a knack for something good. Therefore, why not put it to good use right?

Jokes aside, other than being naturally curious, I *do* take satisfaction in helping people find their families regardless of whatever the outcome ends up being. Knowing what happened to someone you love after they disappeared for any amount of time is better than wondering where they are. Dead or alive.

Twenty painful minutes slowly pass by until our session ends. When we're all getting up to leave, Emma stops me at the door. Through the past year of attending one therapy session per month, Emma is the only person in this group who knows I am a P.I. and also the only one I get along with.

"Hey, if you need a friend to come with you to the cemetery, I don't mind coming with you. Unless you want to be alone or with your husband, I understand," she says.

One bright side of group therapy, you can say I've made my first friend since Chloe died. Emma's sister died from a mugging last year when she was leaving her job late at night which caused Emma to sign up for every form of a self-defense class that she can think of. She's offered for me to attend a karate or kickboxing or one of the many other classes she takes, but I am hesitant to go. Emma and I have gone out to lunch twice already, and that is two times too many for me right now. Given my history with friendships... I don't want this one to end before it even gets started.

Through years of individual and now group therapy, I have come to terms with realizing Laura's death was not my fault. However, getting past Chloe's death is very different. There was nothing that could have made me prevent Laura's car accident because I wasn't in the car with her and if I was, there was nothing I could have done to prevent it either. Thanks to therapy, I've learned how to not blame myself. When it comes to Chloe, I have not come to terms with her death not being entirely my fault and I'm not sure I ever will.

How can I get past the fact that I accused her of being a killer in the first place? And because of my accusation, she ended up dead by the killer who I mistakenly thought she was. How can I just put that in the back of my mind and not blame myself?

"I appreciate the offer but I have some business to take care of when I'm in Avery anyways. I met with a new client this morning and I'm working on looking for his brother," I say as we step out into the parking lot.

"Oh! I'm so happy to hear that!" Emma claps, encouragingly, followed by a smirk. "Well, maybe I shouldn't be happy someone is missing."

Out of everybody in the grief group, I get along with Emma the most. Something about her personality reminds me of my two dead friends. I think both Laura and Chloe would have liked Emma. And I also think Laura and Chloe would have got along with each other too. I guess I'll never know.

"It's kind of ironic how one person's misfortune ends up being my own," I shrug as I think about it. Emma is right. We shouldn't be happy that someone is missing but if someone wasn't missing… then I would be out of a job.

"Want to get lunch right now?" I ask because now I feel bad for turning her down again. I do like Emma and it's hard to shut the woman completely done. Not when she's as caring and persistent as she naturally is. "I was going to stop at the diner for takeout before heading home."

"Works for me!" Emma agrees to meet me there as we begin to walk toward our vehicles.

My phone alerts me with a new text message

from a number with an area code I don't recognize.

Thought I'd be caught by now, huh?

Ding. Another message from the same number appears below it.

You thought wrong.

"Ellie?" Emma's voice causes me to jump.

"Sorry, I uh, actually, I—I have to head home. I have an emergency with my client." I gesture toward my phone. "Lunch next week instead?"

"No problem. Good luck on the case!" Emma smiles.

I thank her and rush over to my truck. I get in, lock the doors, and immediately turn around to check my backseat.

A good rule of thumb when a serial killer is after you, or really just a good rule of safety for anyone: always check your backseat when you get in your vehicle, especially if you're alone. Daylight or not, anyone with malicious intent could be hiding back there.

Once confirming no one is in my backseat, I call the phone number from the text message, keeping my eyes locked on the parking lot around me. Emma just backed out of her spot, and is now driving out toward the road.

"The number you have dialed is not in service." An automated message comes back on the other end of the line.

She either blocked me or she ditched the phone

already… or both.

Unless the person behind these texts isn't the real Tiffany. Detective Carner said she was concerned about copycat killers emerging, yet there haven't been reports of any…

Then again, I haven't spoken to the detective in a couple months now, so maybe there is a copycat out there.

But logically, the sender behind this message can't be a copycat because there are only a handful of people who know about Tiffany's contact to me before: Detective Carner, other law enforcement and my husband.

I scroll over to the last text Tiffany sent me after she murdered Chloe.

Ellie, you and I will reconnect soon.

Is this what she meant by reconnecting? By sending me another cryptic text message two years later to remind me she's still on the run?

5

January 7th
4:30 p.m.

In my house, I rush by Noah who was sitting calmly on the couch watching TV in the living room until I just stormed by.

Once I'm in my office, I immediately pull up the website I utilize for geolocating phone numbers on my computer. I wasn't a private investigator when Tiffany first texted me. Back then, my only resource was to rely on Detective Carner which proved she wasn't of help to me during that time at all. Until I became a P.I, I did not have access to specialized databases for geolocation tracking like I do now.

During my first investigation, I was successful at my first and only attempt in tracking down a missing teenager by her phone number, reuniting her with her family. The teenager, who was hiding out in her boyfriend's house and turned out to be in no danger at all, was not as thrilled about the reuniting. However, her mother who was my paying client, was very satisfied with my services.

"Are you okay?" Noah is standing at the doorway of my office, concern written all over his face. "What's going on?"

Noah cannot start worrying about Tiffany before his meeting tomorrow morning. On the other hand, I promised to not keep anything from him again. Especially when it involves Tiffany.

"Babe?" Noah tilts his head.

"I'm okay. It's just work. I have to look up a phone number." The white lie rolls off my tongue as easily as it had in the past.

"Oh, so your client paid the fee already? Wow. You were right. He is serious about his brother. I'm going to start grilling the burgers outside. Come out whenever you're done," he says as he starts walking away from the doorway.

"Sounds good. I'll be out soon."

Guess I was wrong when I said, no more secrets from my husband.

However, this will be the only one. Eventually, I will tell Noah about the texts once I have more information. There is no sense in having him worry when there is nothing to be done about it. At least, not yet.

Finally, the results for the phone number lookup, load on my screen showing nothing to my avail. There is no owner name or a *find my phone* app linked to the number. Therefore, it's nearly impossible to trace. These messages came from a burner phone just like Detective Carner told me Tiffany used when she texted me years ago. If a phone doesn't have a *find my phone* app downloaded, or if it was bought out of a store instead of a cell phone company, the number is basically untraceable. I move on to identify the phone carrier and network.

My suspicions of it being a burner phone are confirmed. *Wallace Carrier* – a network carrier for prepaid phones.

The area code on the phone number she first texted me from years ago came from Avery. The area code from the message today is from Montana.

Staring at my phone, I think about my promise to Detective Carner. I promised to call her if Tiffany contacted me again… except now I feel like my promise can no longer be valid.

I can't tell the detective about this message. Not yet anyways. If I do, she will end up alerting every law enforcement department. Patrol cars will be parked outside of my property, along with an escort following my every move. None of that will do anyone any good. The presence of law enforcement will draw attention to me and alarm Tiffany that I called them, which is the opposite of a good idea right now.

If we scare Tiffany away, she won't come back for who knows how long and I refuse to let her get away again.

6

TIFFANY

The first man I killed does not usually cross my mind often, but lately he has been swimming around my thoughts for days now. Most times, he appears when I'm busy sleeping.

The memory of the weight of his muscular chest on top of me nearly suffocated my young eighteen-year-old body. I should have taken another shot at the bar before allowing him to take me back to his shitty apartment that night. He thought I drank all of the five shots he bought me before, and by the time we got back to his place, I wished I did. But I had to limit myself because being drunk would not be effective for why I chose to go back home with him that night.

His drunk lips smothered my neck and his hands groped my body underneath my dress as he failed at pulling the next to nothing cloth, over my head. Annoyed with the amount of how much he struggled, I pulled my dress off myself and his lips immediately followed for an attack on my neck.

No, fuck this, I thought. I was not ready to do what I came there for yet. I was a *little too sober* after all. I realized I needed another drink and more importantly, I hadn't located his wallet before we got started. My nights normally never started out like that. I normally scouted out my victims carefully; a sophisticated, yet not too arrogant man, and one who likes to spend at the bar— meaning they have money to spare. Money I could steal without their drunk asses noticing until it was too late. But this time, I judged wrong. Between the shock of his shitty apartment and the absence of his wallet, I was being challenged and I didn't like it.

His wallet was not in the pocket of his pants that he ripped off and left on the floor beside his messy bed. I kicked his jeans before we landed on the sheets and didn't feel it under my feet. I thought, he must have thrown the wallet somewhere in the living room near the front door while he was busy groping me. I needed to know where the wallet was before we proceeded with the night. Even though his apartment had proven he was a waste of my time, I still planned on finding it before we got started. I was already there. Even though his looks deceived me, I was still going to leave with something.

As I had done plenty of times with other men during that year, my strategy was to steal his credit cards and money after having sex with him, then leave as soon as it's over while he's passed out drunk. But everything went wrong that night.

"Wait, I need something to drink," I remember telling him.

"Right now? You need a drink now?" He released his grip around my arms but stayed seated on top of my body. That was the first thing that irritated me. "We're just about to get started," he huffed.

"Get off for a minute," I demanded and he sighed as he reluctantly moved off my body, like my need for another drink caused him a great inconvenience to wait a minute longer.

As I was walking out of the room, he began making himself comfortable in bed with his back to the door, and a sudden sense of rage soared through my body; a rage I never felt until that night.

How dare he try to take advantage of me? First, he misled me by his charisma, swagger, and carelessness of handling his money. Now he was doubting my need to have another drink. I told him to get off me and he questioned me, like I wasn't sure of what I already asked him. And then he sighed like I was causing such a problem, asking him to wait only a couple more minutes before I let him invade my body. He tried to manipulate me into thinking I was going to change my mind from wanting a drink when my mind was already made up. I never liked when a man tries to manipulate me or decides to tell me what to do, especially when he doesn't even know me.

That's when the lamp on his dresser next to the door struck my eye. Without hesitation, I reached over and grabbed hold of it. In a swift swing, I turned around and struck it over the back of his unsuspecting head just as he was getting comfy in bed.

Everything happened so fast. He didn't even scream because he never saw it coming. His body swayed off the left side of the bed and landed on the carpet with a thud. One-hundred and eighty pounds of a useless man unconscious on the floor in a puddle of blood emerging around his head. I was the reason for his pain! For his death, better yet. The new sense of rage that ran through me only moments before drifted into a new high; a high of satisfaction I never wanted to come off of.

I remember thinking, if I knew killing a man would be easy earlier, then he would not have been my first victim. I robbed a few men before him, never thought about killing them though. But that night showed me how simple it actually could be. Men drop their guard for something pretty and I'm gorgeous. All he wanted to do was have sex with me and I was going to let him like I had done so many times with other men before, as long as I got what I wanted in return.

When I left the idiot in his apartment that night, I did panic at first because surely, the cameras in the bar we met at must have caught me with him and soon, I'd be questioned about his death because I was the last one to be seen with him… right?

Wrong. Days turned into weeks that went by after that night and nothing happened to me when my anxiety finally calmed down. And suddenly, I wanted to feel that invigorating feeling again. I got away with it once. It would be easy to do it again.

After killing him, I finally found his wallet which had only about fifty bucks and two credit cards left in it. That was also the night I decided it was time to step my game up and go for men in towns outside of the local bars.

Taking advantage of a man who thinks they are going to take advantage of me became exhilarating. Especially the ones who are unsuspecting of my beauty and talents.

Who would ever suspect me; a beautiful skinny tall young lady with no reason to harm a soul?

Nobody. Nobody until Ellie came around.

7

January 8th
5:30 a.m.

Ben Robinson paid the retainer fee only an hour after he left my office yesterday. I would have looked into Cameron's disappearance as soon as I got back home but the texts messages that I received outside of therapy distracted me for the rest of the day. Although I prefer to focus my attention on Tiffany, I cannot allow her to fill my thoughts during work today. My full attention needs to remain on my client. Each minute I'm not working on looking for him, the more time passes and the chances of Cameron being in danger increase.

Before heading out to Avery to go to the cemetery, I take a few minutes to run a background check on Cameron Robinson in my office.

The results on his background report come up clean. There aren't any criminal charges, felonies, or reports of drug abuse leading to an arrest. I gather the time of his drug addiction never led to anything extreme or criminally involved. Unless it did and he just never got caught.

I shift my search from the background check to social media to look up the username that Ben provided me for Cameron's profiles.

On Facebook and Instagram, Cameron sits in the driver seat of a pickup truck in his profile photo. His shirt is covered in paint stains. His biography states: **Cameron Robinson. Twenty-nine years old. Six foot one. Single. Resides in Fairview, Florida. Occupation: handyman**.

I do not see anything on his page that shows an indication of relapsing. Nothing leads me to believe he had plans on leaving town either. A week ago, he posted a photo where he was painting a living room wall the color beige. There aren't any comments besides four 'likes' under the picture.

I switch my attention from my computer to my phone. After dialing the police department, an operator answers on the other line. "Fairview Police."

"Hello, this is private investigator, Ellie Moore. I am calling to request some information about a missing person. His name is Cameron Robinson."

"There is a report in the system, but it was ruled out," the operator responds.

It was ruled out because the police believe he left town on his own will, basing their decision off his history of drug abuse. That shouldn't automatically deem a person unimportant though, especially when their family member is expressing concern about them going missing. As I have said before, don't let the past determine the present.

I already know what the operator is going to say, yet I ask anyways. "What was the reason for ruling it out?"

"The report states suspicion of drug addiction relapse," she answers.

"Is there probable cause to believe he relapsed though?"

"His history with drug addiction is enough probable cause."

The officer's response angers me and doesn't surprise me at the same time. The negligence of the police is what led me to unmasking Tiffany Burnes in the first place. When I stumbled upon the pattern of the missing men in Avery, I immediately noticed the similarities in their disappearances when it came to timing and their last whereabouts. Before showing my observations to the Detective, each missing person's report had been filed and forgotten.

If it were not for me, those men would still be lost in a missing persons database, and their families would have never received any closure in their disappearances. I will not let another police department almost fail another family again especially when it involves my own client.

8

January 8th
8:30 a.m.

On my way to the cemetery, I made a quick stop in Avery's police station to visit Detective Carner who I haven't seen in person in over two years.

"It's been a while since we saw each other." Detective Carner gets up from her chair to greet me when I walk into her office. "How are you doing?"

"I'm fine. I guess my relentlessness did me some good." I show her my P.I. badge even though she is well aware of my new career endeavour because I called her when I first received my license. The last time I stepped foot in this station was when I was forced to sit in a glass room only a few feet away.

"Turns out being a pain in my ass did you some good." Detective Carner smirks. "I'm proud of you."

Being a pain in her ass is putting it lightly. Looking back at that time, if I were in Detective Carner's place, I would have been just as annoyed with my persistence. However, from my perspective I deserved every right to know what was going on in the investigation and I believe I still do.

Let's not forget, I started this investigation after all. Detective Carner is the one who took over after I gave up my evidence board against Tiffany. If it weren't for me, Tiffany wouldn't even be on the police's radar; a fact that I've brought up to the detective shortly after obtaining my license. I requested to work on the case as a freelance investigator, but Detective Carner won't allow it. She says that I am too close to the suspect, therefore it is too personal and dangerous for me to work on it. I think her reason for not wanting me on the case gives me all the reason to be on it, except that argument ended a while ago.

"I actually stopped by here on my way to visit Chloe. Today makes two years," I say.

"Yes, I know. I was going to give you a call later today to see how you were doing." Detective Carner nods.

"I appreciate that. Well, while I'm here, any new leads on the psychopath?" I shift my feet. She knew I was going to ask.

Detective Carner shakes her head. "Nope. You know, I'll call you whenever something new pops up."

Yeah, that I am not too sure of.

"How is everything going with your investigations? Working on anything exciting?"

"Actually, yes. Although, I wouldn't call the case exciting just yet. I'm starting to look into a male disappearance in Fairview. His name is Cameron Robinson. He went missing after going on a date the other night. He has a history of drug abuse which made Fairview's police department believe he relapsed. So, they won't put him in the system as missing."

"Interesting." Detective Carner slowly nods her head. "Do you have any theories as to what could have happened to him?"

"Nothing solid yet." I shrug. "I plan on looking into it when I get back in town."

"I can run a check on him here and see if he's detained or in the system," Detective Carner offers. "What's his name and DOB?"

After I give her Cameron's information to search through the system, unfortunately, she begins shaking her head. "I'm not finding anything."

"At least you tried. Thanks anyways." I get up to shake her hand. "I'm off to visit Chloe."

I walk out of the detective's office, and pass by the small holding room surrounded by glass windows I once sat in with Chloe the night we saved Jake.

A flashback of Noah yelling my name frantically from the entrance sparks my memory as I walk out of the lobby. If I answered his calls and text messages back then, he would not have come running into the police station to report me missing. Seeing me and Chloe behind the glass windows with a detective in front of us was the last of what he was expecting to happen when he arrived. Have I mentioned, what a saint my husband is?

In the parking lot, my head is on a constant swivel. I remain alert and aware of my surroundings, taking notice of each vehicle and person in the area as I walk to my truck. A silver Lexus with tinted windows is parked directly in front of where I parked. No one is inside though. There is a man sitting in a black SUV that is parked three spots to the left of me. A woman walks to her car, five vehicles over.

Meanwhile, I keep my right hand firmly on my taser that I keep attached to my key ring, and a plan in mind to reach for my gun in my purse with my other hand. I have spent the past few years preparing and training myself to be ready for Tiffany at any given moment. Not just in my house, but everywhere I go in public too.

9

January 8th
9:30 a.m.

My stomach churns as I step over the wet grass toward Chloe's grave. The guilt I have been trying to learn how to surpass is rising in me as I approach a grey inground tombstone with the name, *Chloe Jones*.

"I can't believe you've been gone this long." Without caring that the ground is damp from the storm this morning, I sit down on the grass in front of her name. "Sorry it took me this long to come back here." Gulping, I muster up the words my therapy sessions have been telling me I need to say out loud for a while now. "And I'm sorry I let this happen to you. I'm sorry I brought you into everything. We both know you would still be alive if it weren't for me and my insanity. Sorry it took me a year to apologize to you. I-I…"

I don't know what else to say and can't anyway because my tears are taking over. The sorrow is coming from both a place of guilt and missing her. It's ironic how death can inadvertently make the living feel guilty whether it's the livings' fault or not.

Through all the blame, I try to remind myself that in an ironic turn of events, had it not been for me bringing Chloe into my mess, I never would have uncovered who Avery's serial killer truly was in the first place.

Minutes pass when suddenly being the only person in the cemetery starts to freak me out. Eerie but appropriate silence fills the air. The atmosphere is supposed to be quiet here and that should make me feel comfortable, yet it doesn't.

The entire cemetery is in my view from where I sit in front of Chloe's grave. Nobody is here except me and a couple of a hundred dead bodies buried beneath the ground.

They say you should never be scared of the dead and more so of the living…

I know I am alone. Yet still, my instincts tell me to keep my taser ready. Better be safe than sorry.

Before heading back to my truck, I walk about fifty feet across the cemetery to another grave, my childhood best friend—*Laura Freeman*. A slick wet road sent Laura's car spinning into a guardrail, killing her on impact. Learning to make new friends after her death had been a challenge for me until I met Chloe. Although our friendship came to be under unconventional circumstances, she was my first, true and only friend after Laura died.

Ironically, the two closest friends I have ever had in my life both died and are buried in the same cemetery. Then again, when there are only two cemeteries in this small town, it isn't such a coincidence to be buried in the same place after all. If I were still living here in Avery, I would probably be buried in this cemetery too.

"I know it's been a while since I stopped by," I say, kneeling in front of Laura's grave.

The last time I visited Laura was during Chloe's funeral. I stopped by here for a brief moment to see her after the service was over. More tears flow down my face and again, the words I want to say become stuck in my throat.

Maybe I wasn't ready to come back and see my friends after all.

Again, the eerie feeling of being alone is starting to creep up on me. After a few more minutes of staring at Laura's name, I tell her I miss her and I'll be back when I can.

This is too much for me right now and something's telling me to get back to my truck.

A few feet from approaching the driver's side, I duck down to look underneath the undercarriage to make sure nobody, especially Tiffany, is hiding beneath my vehicle and ready to slash at or grab my ankles.

Confirming no one is there, I unlock my truck with my key fob, then get in, and immediately turn around to look in the backseat.

All clear.

While locking the doors and turning on the ignition, I take another detailed look around the cemetery.

Nobody is around. Not even a gardener or a landscaper. I'm the only one here and have been since I pulled in about fifteen minutes ago.

Now that I feel more relaxed in the safety of my

truck, I back out of the small parking lot. When turning right out of the exit of the cemetery, a text notification alerts me from my phone.

At the next stop sign a hundred feet to the right of the cemetery, I pick up my phone from the cupholder.

Ding. Another message appears.

Ding. Then another.

Three unread text messages appear on my screen from a different unrecognizable number.

It's about time you visit Chloe again. You only live an hour away from Avery. I thought you were a better friend than that. It's not like you're too busy with your new job.

I noticed Noah doesn't travel anymore. I hope I didn't have something to do with that.

I'm proud of you for visiting our friend. After all, you are the reason she is dead anyway.

1 0

"Go around!" I yell out of my window at the man who is honking in the car behind me as he drives around my truck and goes through the stop sign. I remain parked as I call the number from the text message.

"The number you have dialed is not in service."

I can rule out the thought of someone impersonating Tiffany in these messages because this is exactly what she did last time. She sent lengthy paragraphs and multiple texts, then immediately blocked my number…which means she's nearby, watching me.

Or she's tracking my vehicle.

The only two places that are in the line of sight from the cemetery are the gas stations about half a mile to the left of the cemetery behind me.

According to google, the area code on this number comes from Jacksonville, a city six-hours northeast of Fairview. Since the area code from the message yesterday came from Montana, I presume she is using multiple burner phones. Multiple phones with different area codes makes it harder for me to track down which stores they were bought out of it and where she is.

I turn around at the stop sign to quickly pull into the first gas station that is on the right side of the road. I take notice of two vehicles. One is parked in a spot right in front of the store and nobody is inside of it. The other vehicle is parked at the gas pump. No one is pumping gas.

I get out of my truck with my flashlight on my phone, and crouch down to scan every inch underneath my vehicle. There is no type of tracker or air tag anywhere which means Tiffany *is* nearby.

I view my surroundings carefully before running into the store of the gas station. I don't see her anywhere… and I don't see her across the street at the other gas station either. The only car over there is parked on the side of building designated for the employee. I turn around to go into the store behind me.

There are two men in line at the register.

"Excuse me, I have an emergency." I step in front of the customer at the window to talk to the attendant behind the counter. "I'm a local private investigator and I believe the person I'm investigating was just here. Did a woman just come in your store, about five foot eight? Thin? Maybe wearing heels, and a lot of makeup? In her twenties?"

The attendant shakes his head. "No, not recently."

"I need you to show me your security cameras." I quickly pull out my investigative license because I know he is going to ask for some type of credentials.

Once he assesses that my license is real and not fake, not that he would know what a real or fake one looks like because unless you are a private investigator or some type of law enforcement, it is not that easy to tell whether a badge is fake or not, he tells me to wait for him to ring up the two customers that I barged in front of.

I step outside of the entrance to look around the gas station until the customers leave the store. The same two vehicles remain parked outside. A green Mazda is parked at the gas pump. The untinted windows tell me no one is inside. A yellow SUV is parked in front of the store in a parking space. I assume the two customers in line are the owners of those vehicles. A white pick-up truck that is the same model as mine, is pulling up to one of the three gas pumps here. A man steps out to pump his gas while a woman remains sitting in the passenger seat on her phone. By the color of her skin, look of age, and facial features, I confirm that she is not the psychopathic woman who just texted me.

Tiffany may change identities and her physical appearance but there are certain things she can't change if you know what to look for.

I look across the street again at the other gas station. Three young women who look to be between sixteen to eighteen just got out of their car. Two of them go into the store, while one stays outside to pump gas. All of them are too young to be Tiffany.

Once the two men walk out of the store behind me, I rush back inside to talk to the attendant again.

"I'm sorry but this is urgent. Can you please,

hurry?" I ask, tapping my foot wildly on the floor.

After the attendant quickly scrubs through the past twenty minutes of camera footage, we see a blue truck drive into the parking lot, and parks at a gas pump just a couple of minutes after I got to the cemetery. A woman gets out of the driver's side to pump her gas but I don't bother taking note of her license plate because she isn't Tiffany. Her physical appearance is significantly different just alone by age.

Eight minutes after the woman leaves in the blue truck, a red Toyota sedan with tinted windows suspiciously drives up to a gas pump. The car remains parked for fourteen minutes before driving away.

"Pause that and play it back please," I tell the attendant.

During the fourteen minutes, the driver never leaves the vehicle. They remain parked for the remainder of the time I was at the cemetery. Two minutes before I received the text, the car drives away. Instead of asking for a copy of this footage, I film the monitor with my phone and zoom in on the license plate because that's all I need. Then I thank the attendant for his help, leaving my business card with him.

I am ninety percent certain, the person in the red car was Tiffany because the timing of the vehicle suspiciously parking there while I was at the cemetery and the driver never getting out, is not a coincidence. However, I like to cover my tracks so I am heading to the other gas station to question the attendant in the store over there as well.

When I walk inside, the three teenagers are gone and this cashier is more hesitant to show me his security cameras. Instead of being immediately helpful, he facetimes his boss who I show my license to over the phone.

Once they are both satisfied in wasting my time, the attendant plays back the last hour of footage. The video shows two male customers pumping gas into their vehicles at different times before I arrived at the cemetery. Nobody was at this gas station during the time I was there, leaving me to further believe Tiffany was in the red Toyota.

Still, I film what is on the monitor with my phone, zooming in on each license plate anyways. On my way home, I will make a call to Detective Carner. When I said I have law enforcement connections, I consider the detective my go-to. She may not excel in finding missing persons, but I think she can handle a few simple license plate lookup requests.

1 1

Ellie's admiration for men is sickening as I watch her run around town to look for a man named Cameron who she doesn't even know. She cares way too much for the male gender which I cannot even begin to fathom.

I could have killed her the same night I killed Chloe, but what fun would that be if I didn't get to torment her first? Having Ellie live her life in fear is more impactful. Let her worry about when I'd strike again. Who would I kill and would she be next? And clearly, my plan to keep her living in fear worked. It just took longer than I originally intended.

Oh, Ellie. Now that you're a private investigator, you think you can still outwit me?

No matter where Ellie went, I promised I would find her and I did. Once I obtained the knowledge of Ellie's new address in Fairview, I set on an adventure back to Florida. About six months ago, I targeted a wealthy lawyer at a hotel bar when I was living in Montana. I ended up going back to his hotel that night and resisted my urge to end his life.

Throughout the three weeks I spent there, I never left the hotel and when I did, I only did it when the lobby was full of people. In order to not be seen, you have to blend in. I spent my time in his hotel room while he was out at long meetings, and I convinced him to pay for a breast enhancement surgery that he didn't know I never planned on getting.

Once he gave me exactly the amount of cash I asked for, I left his hotel room while he was at work—right at the time of checkout. I moved through the crowded lobby, and avoided the security cameras effortlessly.

Even though I had enough money to catch a flight, get a car rental, or even hop on the train, my only source of transportation without getting ID checked was a disgusting public bus. I didn't even make it out of Montana when the feeling of eyes started to pierce my back and I realized public transportation was too risky.

Stealing vehicles along the way, just long enough to get me from place to place would be a better idea. I've stolen a car a few times as a teenager, so why not do it again?

Back then, I was a stupid kid without thoroughly thinking my actions through. Now as an adult, I can say I'm much wiser now.

Ellie and I have a love-hate relationship. I can thank Ellie for the opportunity to live on the other side of the country. But although I grew accustomed to living in the Midwest, it feels nice to be back in the sunshine state: my home. I wish it were an option for me to stay and live here for good.

I miss stability—being able to return home to the same bed every night, my own bed. Not a hotel room or a random man's bed.

It would even be nice to go back to my old house in Avery, maybe even drive over to Jonesville to catch up with Billie and Dianne. That is, if Dianne's around. But all of that is no longer a reality for me anymore. Ellie took my stability away and for that, I hate her.

On the other hand, I thank her again for giving me the chance to overcome a new challenge. I had been so used to getting rid of men over the years; I had no idea that I was missing out on how invigorating it felt to kill a woman too. When I killed Chloe, I sensed a different form of strength than opposed to what I feel from my male victims.

Seducing and flirting with her was not an option. My looks and my personality couldn't be used as a weapon that night. I needed a plan—a way to outsmart her and I went through with it effortlessly. Chloe would not be dead if it weren't for her impulsive annoying new bestie. Ellie can thank herself for that.

1 2

The few cases that I have worked on over my short time in my new career do not exceed to Cameron's disappearance. A month after I first promoted my services online, my first client came to me in search of her husband which led me to a cheating spouse. She reported him to the police who put him in Fairview's missing persons database, but the police didn't work diligently enough to look for him. When two days went by and she had not heard from her husband or received any updates from the police, she inquired into my services. It only took me a day and a half to find her husband shacked up with another woman in a hotel half an hour away from Fairview.

My second investigation led me to the runaway teenager where I successfully tracked down her whereabouts by geolocating her phone number and staking out the area she was in.

My third client reached out to me regarding her older sister who had been missing for three weeks. The police put her in the system as a missing person, but the department did not put any efforts into searching for her. After two weeks of my own investigation, I followed her sister to an apartment a couple hours away from town. I staked her out and confronted her where she told me she moved in with a new boyfriend. Since she was known to be the black sheep of the family and had a history of multiple arrests for various reasons with previous boyfriends, she feared hearing her family's judgement, so she ignored their calls and messages.

Another potential client reached out to me in search of his cousin who went missing three years ago. Ed, an elderly man hired a list of other investigators in town who all failed him before calling me. I briefly searched for his cousin through my own resources with all of the information he provided me, but had no luck in finding anything, so I decided not to take on his case. If other private investigators with more experience than me couldn't help him, then how would I be able to?

Thinking about it now, I should have challenged myself and at least gave it a shot. Although out of the many things I've learned about missing person cases, as much as I don't like to know this is true; some cases will always remain a mystery.

I don't want Cameron's disappearance to remain a mystery too. I already left a voicemail for Detective Carner regarding a license plate lookup request on the vehicles at the gas stations in Avery. I told her the reasoning for my request pertained to my investigation regarding my current client. I did not tell her that I think Tiffany could have been in any of those vehicles, specifically the red Toyota. Hopefully, she will get back to me with all that information today while I continue to work on finding Cameron.

As a P.I., there are limitations to what I can and cannot do for my clients. If I were working with a lawyer or law enforcement on Cameron's case, I would easily be able to access his bank transactions, phone records, and more. But that does not mean I don't have the resources and capabilities to still get the job done.

I am only able to get Cameron's debit card transactions if Ben were a joint owner on his brother's account. Unfortunately, he isn't. However, if he has access to the login information for Cameron's online banking, then that would be equally useful. It was worth a shot, and a well given one because it turns out, Cameron leaves his username and password auto saved in his computer at home.

It is illegal and immoral for me to look at his bank transactions without legal permission from Cameron himself or his attorney which he does not have. So instead, Ben read them to me over the phone. Call it a loophole, or simply, call it getting the job done but I do not classify this as illegal. As long as my client is okay with my strategy and tactics, then so am I.

According to Ben, Cameron's last purchase took place at 7:32 p.m. in a corner store down the road from their apartment on the fifth—the night he was last seen by Ben before leaving for Angelinos.

"That transaction was probably for the cigarettes he went out to buy before he went on his date," Ben says over the phone. "He walked over to the corner store. Then he came back home and got ready to go to Angelinos."

"So, let me get the timeline of that night straight. What time did Cameron come home from work on the fifth?" I ask while pulling into the entrance of the shopping plaza where Angelinos is.

"He came home from work at around six thirty in the evening. Then he walked to the store to get cigarettes about an hour later. He came back from the store to shower and change his clothes, then he left around eight o'clock for his date."

"Okay, so—"

"Shit. Wait a second!" Ben interrupts me. "It says that his last transaction was at the corner store. That must mean he didn't make it to Angelinos after all… right?" Ben's voice raises with concern. "There's no charge on his card from there. It's been three days. The charge for dinner would show as pending by now, wouldn't it? Something must have happened to him on the way there..."

"Does your brother ever carry cash?" I ask while parking my truck in the parking lot of the shopping plaza. Regardless of what Cameron's last transaction reveals, I am going to request the restaurants security footage to see whether he made it there that night or not.

"He might carry cash sometimes but not often. I've mostly seen him use his debit card whenever we're out together," Ben tells me.

"Okay. I am about to walk into Angelinos now to speak with the manager and see if Cameron made it there with his date. I will call you back when I have more information."

Before I walk through the entrance of the restaurant, I spot a security camera that is mounted to the right corner of the building above the doors.

Once I'm done speaking with the hostess, the manager comes out from the kitchen a few minutes later. He greets me with a handshake. "Hello, my name is Jackson. You requested to speak with me?"

"Yes, hi. My name is Ellie Moore. I am a private investigator for missing persons." I show him my badge. "I am currently searching for a man who ate dinner here around eight-thirty at night on the fifth. I would like to see your security footage to confirm whether or not he made it here."

Without working with an attorney on Cameron's disappearance, it becomes challenging for me to access security footage on my own. However, with the consent of the owner of the establishment where the cameras are set up, I do not need a legal representative for permission to obtain it.

"I can only show the footage to police officers ma'am," Jackson answers hesitantly.

"That's actually not true, sir. My client is missing and he could be in danger. If there is something that your cameras caught that night, it is pertinent I see them. I am just simply asking for your cooperation in bringing my client back home safely to his family." I smile. "Also, it is required by law to provide me with your security footage per my request since my client was reportedly last seen at your business before he went missing. I have probable cause that he was here as well."

I do not have probable cause besides what Ben told me. I only know he had plans to meet here but I do not have any proof of those plans. Hopefully, Jackson doesn't try to call me out on it.

Another moment of hesitancy goes by before Jackson gestures for me to follow him through the kitchen. Then we walk through a door at the end of the hallway leading into his office.

I've learned that most potential witnesses and suspects are hesitant to cooperate with me regardless of whether they are guilty or not. People don't like inserting themselves into situations if they don't need to be. I don't blame them for it, but when it comes to my clientele, I will not back down.

Since Cameron told me Ben left the apartment at eight o'clock, the earliest he should have arrived at Angelinos would be ten minutes later even though his date was scheduled for eight-thirty. I mapped out the directions on my phone from his apartment to Angelinos. It would have only taken him no more than a ten-minute drive without traffic and there shouldn't have been traffic at that time of night. Presuming he left straight from his apartment and didn't stop anywhere along the way, then he should not have arrived any later. I tell Jackson to play me the footage beginning about ten minutes past eight o'clock that night.

At 8:15 p.m., Cameron appears in front of the entrance of the restaurant. "Right there. Pause it. Play those last few frames back, please."

When Jackson replays the video, I confirm it's Cameron when he turns to the side and I see his profile. Six minutes go by as Jackson scrubs through more sped-up footage when a bright red-headed woman, dressed in a slim black fitted dress and black heels to match, greets Cameron with a hug. Her red lips stand out as they match her perfectly red shoulder length wavy hair. After chatting for a moment outside of the restaurant, they turn to look at the big menu in front of the entrance.

Two minutes later, it looks like they decide to choose not to walk into Angelinos. Instead, they take a left down the sidewalk, walking out of the security camera's view.

"They must've decided to go to Joe's pizza next door," Jackson says as he stands up from his desk. "Or maybe the burger place that's further down in the plaza. I'm sorry, ma'am. I really need to get back out on the floor to help my servers. We're short staffed in the kitchen and it's lunch hour. Can I help you with anything else?"

"Can you please email me all the footage you just showed me before you go back out there?" I request, remaining in my seat. He takes my card with my email and quickly types away at his desk.

Once I confirm retrieval of his email with the video files attached, I thank him, then head to the pizza place next door.

1 3

January 8th
1:30 p.m.

Opposed to the manager at Angelinos, Lexie who is the owner of Joe's pizzeria, did not hesitate to help me at all. On her computer, I watch Cameron and his date walk through the entrance of her restaurant at 8:24 p.m. I ask Lexie to show me the security camera footage from the dining area after that. She switches over to the dining room camera and scrubs over to the time they walked in.

A hostess leads Cameron and his date to a booth in the far-left corner of the dining room.

"Pause it," I tell Lexie, so I can get a better look at the woman's face.

Her red shoulder length hair and perfectly square bangs across her forehead looks like a wig which is what Tiffany is known to disguise herself with. But other than that, there is no resemblance to each other. The height difference between the woman on camera and Cameron who is six-foot tall, is impeccable. Tiffany is five foot eight. Cameron's date looks like she is about five foot five as she stands next to him and her high heels look to be at least an inch tall. This confirms that I can rule Tiffany out as the identity of Cameron's date but is this woman responsible for his disappearance?

When they sit down in the booth, Cameron chooses the seat that faces the lobby. His date sits with her back toward the camera facing him.

"Do you have another camera that is closer to their booth?"

"No. This is the closest one," Lexie answers.

After fast forwarding through thirty minutes of footage of Cameron and his date eating dinner, their waitress comes by to drop off the check. Cameron begins to take his wallet out of his back pocket.

"Pause it right here. I need to see what he used to pay the bill."

Cameron pulls cash out from his wallet before sliding it in the black book and handing it back to the waitress. It seems like he told her to keep the change because right after he pays, he and his date get up from the booth and begin walking toward the exit.

"Can you switch back to the outdoor camera so I can see which way they went after they left here?" As Lexie switches the cameras over, I pull out my business card to give her.

At 9:40 p.m., we watch Cameron and his date leave the pizzeria. Then they walk out to the right, down the sidewalk toward the other businesses in the plaza and where the parking lot is.

I ask Lexie to send me a copy of the footage to my email. After confirming retrieval of her email, I thank her and continue my impromptu afternoon walk toward the parking lot where my truck is.

I need to get in contact with the company that surveillances this plaza and that is going to be tricky. Surveillance companies aren't very privy to private investigators without an attorney or police officer present. They are also not so easy to swindle like I did with the cashiers at the gas stations in Avery and Jackson and Lexie here in this plaza either. By law, whoever covers the parking lot should oblige, given the circumstance of Cameron's case. I have evidence this was the last location of his whereabouts by the security cameras at both restaurants.

As I pass two other restaurants, an ice cream place and three bars, I spot four security cameras in the plaza. There isn't a security booth or a sign with the company's name anywhere though.

When I reach the parking lot, I look for more cameras until I spot one that is mounted up on a street lamp in the corner of the lot, but there is no sign with the surveillance company's name on the pole or beneath the camera. Since I had a more pleasant experience with Lexie, I'm going to walk back in the pizzeria and ask her for the companies contact information. On the way, I'll stop in the ice cream place and the bars to request to see their security footage on the night of the fifth too. Maybe Cameron and his date went to get a drink at one of the bars after eating dinner. Just because he was addicted to cocaine in the past might not mean an alcoholic drink is out of the question. I have to rule out all possibilities.

When I'm turning around to walk out of the parking lot back toward the plaza again, a flash of red catches the corner of my right eye…

A man in a bright red T-shirt is running toward me. Instinctively, I go for my taser but his friendly smile stops me from grabbing hold of it, and I realize he isn't running directly at me.

He's waving at another woman in the parking lot behind me.

I need to relax and focus on my job. The color red is messing with my head because I am associating it with the red Toyota that I saw at the gas station in Avery. Which speaking of the red car, Detective Carner needs to get back to me soon before I call her again. It's only been a few hours since I left her a voicemail, but my patience is starting to wear thin. I could call Fairview's department to request a lookup on the license plates, but I am not so keen on working with them since they dismissed Ben about Cameron's disappearance so quickly.

I am also heavily on edge since I know Tiffany is nearby which is not helping any with my patience. She followed me all the way to Avery, so I have to assume she must be watching me right now. After all, I shouldn't put anything past her at this point. Just like she learned not to put anything past me.

1 4

January 8th
3:30 p.m.

The manager at the ice cream place resisted when I asked to see his camera footage, but he did give me the name of the security company for the plaza; Asset Surveillance systems. Since the security company has a local office in Fairview, I drove straight here. After I showed the videos of Cameron from Joes and Angelinos to the manager here, he adhered to my request.

At 8:12 p.m., a black F-150 truck pulls into a parking spot that matches Cameron's license plate. A minute later, he gets out of the truck alone, then walks out of the lot toward the plaza.

We fast forward to 9:40 p.m. Eight minutes later, Cameron is seen walking back to his truck. This time, with his date by his side. He opens the passenger door for her before getting in the driver's side. A moment later, he backs the truck out of the spot, then turns left when exiting the parking lot.

My assumption is that he drove his date back

home to her place and stayed the night since Ben said he didn't come home, and that is what he speculated happened with his brother in the first place. The date probably went well as it seems to have looked like it did from what I saw of their interaction through all the security footage. Or as I thought of before, they could have gone out for drinks, maybe even coffee, or dessert, but somewhere outside of the plaza instead.

"Can you please email me a copy of this footage? Everything from between eight o'clock to ten o'clock that night?"

Somebody could have been waiting for Cameron and followed him out of the plaza when they left after dinner. Was Tiffany parked in the red car or in another vehicle, watching him like she was watching me at the cemetery? Or was someone else watching him and did they follow him out of the plaza? Did his date set him up?

When I get back to my office, I will replay those hours to focus closely on Cameron's surroundings in the parking lot. Now that I can confirm Cameron met the woman in person, my next step is to track her down.

On my way home, I make a call to Ben so that he can stay updated. "Hi. Ben. How are you doing today?"

"I'm hanging in there. Hoping you got some good news for me, huh?"

"Well, not bad news. I have tracked Cameron's last whereabouts on the night he disappeared. He met his date outside of Angelinos but then decided to have dinner at Joes, another restaurant in the plaza. He paid for their dinner with cash and left with his date a few minutes past a quarter to nine. Now, I wanted to ask you about the dating app he was using to meet women again. Are you sure you don't know what it's called? Maybe there's a note or something in his room that might have the name or possibly, the name of his date. Maybe you could look at his computer again."

"Honestly, I really can't remember what the app is called if he told me, but his coworkers might know. He's around them all day. He might have told them more than what he told me," Ben answers. I can hear a tone of fault and anger toward himself because he can't better help in answering my questions.

"Can you give me the contact information to his boss or any of those coworkers?"

"I can text you his boss's information," Ben says. "I already called and told him that I hired a P.I so when you call, he won't give you a hard time. I forgot to tell you, I looked at my brother's messages on Facebook after I went through his bank statements because he left his account logged in. I can't get into his Instagram but there was nothing on his Facebook about his date or anything."

"Oh, great job! Thank you. I'll be in touch after I speak with his coworkers."

Ben has already told me that he and Cameron are on separate phone plans. If they were on a family plan, he would be able to see what apps are downloaded on all of the devices under the plan. If that were the case, I would be able to easily find the dating app and track down the red headed woman Cameron was last seen with.

But nothing is ever easy in life, right?

1 5

January 8th
4:45 p.m.

Over the phone, Cameron's boss gave me the address of his employee's current job site.

The three handymen who usually work with Cameron were able to tell me the name of the dating app he was using—*Lovestruck*. When I asked what his coworkers thought of Cameron's disappearance, they were all shocked to find out the news. They figured he was sick the past few days. When I asked if they had any suspicions of him relapsing or leaving town, they believed that none of those possibilities could be true. His boss also informed me that it wasn't like Cameron to not show up for work without calling to let him know. He called Cameron three times on the morning of the sixth because he was scheduled to clock in for work that day. The phone went to voicemail every time.

Now with the knowledge of the name of the dating app, I am one step closer to finding out who his red-headed date is. First, I call Ben again.

"I just spoke with Cameron's coworkers. They

told me that your brother was on a dating app called *lovestruck*. Now that I know the name, I need to get into Cameron's account to contact the woman who he was last seen with. I can only do that by getting into his messages, so I need to hack into his profile. I just wanted to ask your permission before I proceed. If you don't mind, I will need his email, along with any phrases and words you can think of that he uses for passwords. You said, you were able to get into his Facebook the other day. Maybe you can figure out his password for Lovestruck that way. Since his info is already saved on the login screen, there should be a backup of his passwords somewhere in his browsers account. If you need help figuring it out, I can show you how to find it through a video call."

"Oh, no problem!" Ben answers. "Wow, you work quick! I truly appreciate it. Do what you need to. Do whatever it takes. I'm on my way home now. As soon as I get there, I'll check it out and call you."

I could use all of the same information Ben finds to login any other of Cameron's social media profiles besides Facebook and Lovestruck, and other pertinent accounts such as his banking, and insurance information, really anything that will lead me to locating him. But again, without legal representation and assistance on the case, I can only do so much. While I'm not one to shy away from bending the rules, jeopardizing my investigative license is the last outcome I desire. Private investigation is where I belong, and it's where I'll stay.

Some investigators would not work as quickly on a case like I am working on Cameron's because the longer it takes to find someone; the more money the client has to shell out. Some investigators like to use that time to their advantage. But the longer a case takes to solve, the longer a person remains missing which leads to more chances of them being in danger or ending up dead. I am not in this career for the money. At least, not entirely. I chose to be a P.I. after I realized I was good at solving mysteries, and I like bringing families back together— no matter what gender or background they come from.

Back in my office, I make countless attempts to hack into Cameron's *lovestruck* profile, using various options of the password that he uses for his Facebook. Twenty minutes later, when I am on my fifth attempt of a variation, I'm successful at logging in. In his most recent chat, there is a message from *Vee B. Age 27. Height 5'6.* Their last conversation took place the morning of the fifth, confirming they would meet later that night at eight-thirty in front of Angelinos.

Vee's profile photo only shows her face from the neck up. The color of her hair is red, matching the same style it was on the security footage with Cameron. However, she doesn't have any bangs in this photo.

As I compare her picture to the woman on the videos at Joes, Angelinos and in the parking lot, I conclude this is definitely the same person. Either she wears red wigs or this photo of her on Lovestruck was taken before she cut her bangs.

While awaiting an image search result on Google using her profile photo, I send her a message.

C: Hey! How's it going?

I scroll through the first two pages of results from the image search, and I find two social media accounts that look like a match. When clicking on the first result, a notification from Lovestruck appears on my phone.

V: Good. You?

C: Same. I enjoyed our first date. Would you like to meet for a second?

Out of the two plausible profiles that seem to be a match to her photo, the second one is what I'm looking for. Just as I am clicking on the link, a knock on my office door distracts me.

"Come in," I call out to Noah.

"Hey, I have a meeting in twenty minutes, so you know where I'll be. When I'm done, do you want to go out and get dinner somewhere tonight?"

I want to say yes, but the thought of leaving my house at night unattended is suddenly very unsettling to me. Even with the confidence in my surveillance cameras and alarm system, I don't want to leave my house at night, knowing that Tiffany is nearby. She followed me to Avery so I have to assume she followed me from my own home…

"Sure." I nod, forcing a smile.

"What's wrong?" Noah tilts his head.

No more secrets from my husband.

"I'll tell you after your meeting. Don't worry." I smile.

Noah needs to remain concentrated on his meeting before I tell him that Tiffany texted me, let alone has proven she's nearby. My decision to switch career paths from a bill collections agent to private investigation did not come shocking to him. However, it took him some time getting used to. Working from home however, Noah took to getting used to perfectly fine. "It's the same as working in an office except I don't have to wear pants when I'm in a meeting. This is my dream," Noah likes to say when it comes to his change in work environment.

He is happier to be home, just not as ecstatic about the pay cut. Neither of us are. It's not that we are short on bills. Financially, we are able to get by comfortably. Just not as comfortably as we were used to before I brought Tiffany into our lives.

Along with the slight dip in finances, our freedom of feeling safe in public and at home, the fact that she killed my friend because of me, and then ran me out of my hometown; you can see why there are a list of many reasons I want the woman dead and not just behind bars.

1 6

TIFFANY

"So, where are you from?" A charming blue-eyed man whose name I have not asked for and do not plan on it, just ordered me my third shot. He's not my normal target, yet I still decide to humor him. These days I have to take what I can get, thanks to Ellie.

"I'm from everywhere. Call me a traveller," I respond before shooting back the shot of rum. As much as I want to keep feeling the burn of the alcohol down my throat, this is my limit. No more drinking for me if I decide to see this through tonight.

My taste of men is not usually found in this type of bar which is why I chose to come here. I'm good with money for now so targeting someone isn't needed. I just wanted to come here to lay low until the rain lets up, then I will find a hotel and sleep for the night.

But this man. This man is persistent. Persistently annoying which makes him an easy target—easy for me not to resist.

"I like a mysterious woman." He leans in closer to me, his cologne overpowering my air.

"Everyone likes a mystery." I whip my long black curls over my shoulder, the black of my hair blending in with the color of my dress.

Being a woman is amazing. We have multiple ways to change our appearance as opposed to the choices men have. All that's needed for us to look different are wigs, makeup, and a wardrobe of variety.

"Want to get out of here?" The green snake tattoo on Mr. Blue eyes right arm strikes my eye as he brings the shot to his lips.

I remember when my nights would begin as simple as this. I'd draw the attention of an attractive male at work. We would flirt the whole night and he'd fill me with drinks while I pretend to be drunker than what I really am. By the end of my shift in the club and in the bars, I would find myself in his bed or whatever bed he lies about being his.

This persistently annoying man with the snake tattoo is the opposite from the men in my past. Thanks to Ellie, everyone knows that I normally go for younger. But maybe this older guy is a better choice for the night since my usual target is not in this bar anyways. Might as well take what I can get which has been months since my last encounter.

"Where do you want to take me?" With my long black painted finger nail, I rub the green ink on his arm. Since I've had to go incognito over the years, my nail game has been downgraded to press-on nails instead of getting a professional manicure done at the salon; Another inconvenience on me due to Ellie's antics.

"I have a place we can go to for the night. It's down the road." He leans in even closer which seemed impossible until now. His thigh is practically on top of mine. He shoots back another shot, wobbling slightly to the side.

For the night. He is inferring to a place that isn't his which means he most likely isn't single. He probably does this often: I bet he hits on and picks up women at the bar to cheat on his wife or girlfriend. There is no ring indentation on his finger but then again, he might take the ring off so often, that there isn't one anymore.

"Lead the way." I reach my hand out for the green snake to lead me out of the bar.

Down the road, he parks in front of a motel 8; a seedy two-story building that is only a five-minute drive from the bar we were just in. Next to the motel, there is a small shopping plaza which is thankfully closed since it's after one o'clock in the morning.

"Ready?" Mr. Blue eyes yells over the loud rain that is slamming against the car windows.

I'm more ready than you think I am, buddy.

Without answering him, I open the door and rush out into the rain to the hotel. The convenience of the rain and that it's the middle of the night allows me less chances of getting seen by anyone. Whoever owns the two cars in the parking lot are hopefully sound asleep in their motel rooms. The motel office is all the way on the other side of the room that we're starting to walk to and there are no cameras in the hallways either. *This is perfect.*

I used to plan out my attacks on my victims

accordingly, but since Ellie made me famous, I've had to adapt to every situation. I can no longer kill the way I used to kill; the way I truly enjoyed.

Also most importantly, I cannot bury my victims with the certainty of knowing they would never be found. Instead of taking comfort in knowing where the bodies are buried, now it is important that I make their deaths look like an accident— a calculated way of dying, leaving my victims where they took their final breath. It is all too exhausting for me. Until Ellie came around and ruined everything, killing used to be more fun.

Although being famous comes with its downfalls, I do enjoy knowing that the public knows my name. Along with a list of other talented individuals, I belong in the same group of the most prolific and proficient famous serial killers. Think BTK, Aileen Wuornos, The Golden State killer, Jeffery Dahmer and then me, Tiffany Burnes.

I have even heard my name in conversations a few times over the years. All the way in Montana! It was a challenge to fight the temptation to jump into the conversation and ask for an autograph.

Imagine being in public, and you're talking to somebody about a wanted serial killer. Then all of a sudden, the stranger beside you in the supermarket interrupts and says, "Hi! You're talking about me! Want an autograph?"

Now, wouldn't that be something to talk about?

1 7

I spent the entire night going through the parking lots security footage from Assets surveillance company. I never spotted Tiffany or anyone else lurking around Cameron's surroundings when he arrived to the parking lot or when he left with his date that night. A few hours passed by when the cracks and noises from this old house were enough to distract me from staring at the screen, so I shifted my search over to look for Vee.

Another reason for not liking this house as much as the one in Avery; the noises here are noticeably vocal at night. Then again, this house is a lot older than our previous one. I can't ask for perfect.

The image search of Vee's profile photo from lovestruck, led me to the same picture that was posted a few months ago on her Facebook page. In her current profile photo there, she looks more like the woman who was seen eating dinner with Cameron at Joes.

Her Facebook posts tell me that she works in the evenings; Monday through Friday because she often posts complaints about being there in the moment.

A photo of her in work uniform is posted at 4:00 p.m. on January 7th at the grocery store with the caption – *Five more hours and I'm free.*

Yesterday, she wrote: *Can't wait for my shift to end!* at 5:30 p.m.

Today is a weekday. Therefore, she must be scheduled to work a shift this evening. If she doesn't reply to Cameron's message soon, I will pay her a visit at her job later on.

As I sip my third cup of coffee, I think about what Detective Carner told me over the phone last night. Before I began looking through the parking lots footage, she surprised me with some informative news regarding my requests for the license plate number lookups out of Avery. The two vehicles at the second gas station were registered to their rightful owners, but the plate on the Red Toyota at the first gas station came back as a stolen vehicle out of Montana. The owner reported the car as stolen to the police two months ago when he came out of a shopping mall and did not find his car where he left it parked. The parking lots security camera did not catch the thief. However, I am ninety percent sure Tiffany was the person who was behind the wheel.

The first number she texted me from came back as a Montana area code. The burner phone and the stolen car both being from the same state cannot be a coincidence. I surmise after Tiffany bought the phone in Montana, she then stole the car out of the busy shopping mall and used it to drive down to Florida. She must have bought another burner phone in Jacksonville on her way to Avery. Whether she is still behind the wheel of the red car or whether she already ditched it by now, I can't be sure.

And if she stole it two months ago, then I have to assume she's been around longer than only a few days.

Ditching the vehicle after sending the text message would have been a smart move on her part, especially after revealing how close in proximity she was to me. But would Tiffany be so ignorant to put my work as a P.I. by me? Did she not think I would utilize my resources to find her? Maybe she just underestimated me again like she admitted in her lengthy text message the night she killed Chloe.

I made a mistake; thinking you two weren't as smart as you are.

Then again, Tiffany has already acknowledged to making that mistake before, so there is no way she would make it again. Either she wanted me to see her in the red car or she overlooked my capabilities as an investigator.

As for her recent messages, it's important to note there has been no mention of Cameron. That leads me to believe the timing of Cameron's disappearance and Tiffany's return might just be a coincidence after all. If Tiffany were behind his disappearance, she would boast about it. Just as she did when she killed Chloe. Besides, realistically, how would it be possible for her to know that Ben would reach out to me and not any of the other few private investigators in this town anyway? There's absolutely no way to know he would choose me. Therefore, Tiffany shouldn't be responsible for Cameron's disappearance. It wouldn't make sense.

Shifting my focus to the thread of text messages

Tiffany sent to me the night she killed Chloe; I'm reminded of the past when re-reading her words.

I wanted to personally say goodbye and thank you for what you did for me. Ellie, you are the reason I tried something new!

Killing a female wasn't as satisfying as killing a male but, in this case, I was happy to do it. So happy that I think I will do it again! It's enthralling to take advantage of a man. However, I never knew how equally enticing it would be to take advantage of a woman too. I thank you for that, Ellie. You opened up a whole new experience for me!

Tiffany thanked me for a "new experience" but her life isn't the same as it was before, and I know she can't be happy about that.

Her life isn't as simple as it used to be— killing her victims, then burying them in her own backyard without worrying that someone could find them or suspect that she is responsible for their disappearances.

Just like my life got forcibly uprooted, hers did too.

We fuel the same rage toward each other, but the difference between us— she wants revenge on me and I just want her dead.

She wants to torture me instead. A quick or gruesome death is not the perfect revenge. It's fear which is what she's been keeping me in ever since she killed Chloe.

Nevertheless, I can't forget, I outsmarted her before. Then it shouldn't be difficult to do it again.

I just have to think like her again: *I have to think like a killer.*

It's up to her when she wants me to text back. That is, if she wants me to text back which seemingly, she doesn't. If I can't respond to her messages, then she is the only one who stays in control of the situation. I'm the only one that remains kept on edge, living in fear.

But since I can't contact her directly, I can indirectly reach out to her online. If Tiffany is watching me as closely as she says she is, then I can guarantee she is keeping track of my social media presence which has been almost non-existent until right now.

I set my phone up against the lamp on my desk in selfie mode before hitting record.

"Hi, everyone. My name is Ellie Moore. I am a private investigator out of Fairview, Florida and I specialize in finding missing persons. I have never spoke in detail about my involvement regarding Tiffany Burnes; the wanted serial killer who came out of Avery, Florida only a few years ago, but I feel like today is appropriate. Three years ago, I began my own investigation in seeking out several men who were listed in the missing persons database while I was living in Avery. After countless weeks of theorizing a pattern between the male disappearances, my conclusion led me to Tiffany Burnes. I then, took my evidence against her to Avery's police department where they reviewed my findings which prompted them to open up a criminal investigation. While my involvement ended quite shortly after bringing attention to my findings, I've continued searching for Tiffany Burnes on my own without the assistance of the police since then. And that is why I am reaching out to the public today. If anyone would like to reach out with any tips or sightings of

Tiffany, please don't hesitate to contact me. My information is in my bio. Anybody who calls in a tip will remain anonymous. And if Tiffany Burnes is watching this, I want you to know that I still believe you will get what's coming to you. You can't hide out forever."

After stopping the video on my phone, I post it to both my Facebook page and Instagram that is created for my business.

Other than what is written on my website in order to gain clientele, I never spoke about my involvement in the Tiffany Burnes case publicly until this video. Hopefully, I won't regret hitting post just now.

1 8

Shamefully, I thought my video would gain some form of traction on the internet, except there have been no new comments underneath the post yet. Only six likes, and a couple wow emoji reactions. And most importantly, no new text from Tiffany yet.

It has only been a couple hours since the post though, so my hopes remain high. Hopefully, she sees the video, realizing that I outwitted her by utilizing social media to give her a response, let her know I am receiving her messages and they do not scare me. There is no way she will let my response go unnoticed whenever she does see the video because it's not in her character to keep that information to herself. When the timing is right, she brags about what she's done; when she feels that she is safe enough to confess her crimes and boasts about them at the same time.

While I await a response out of Tiffany, I focus my attention on Vee. She messaged Cameron back on Lovestruck yesterday evening, and agreed to meet with him for lunch today. I knew her work schedule began in the evening, so I persuaded her into meeting for lunch at Capone's pizzeria beforehand.

"Heading out?" As I am grabbing my purse off my dresser in the bedroom, Noah walks in from the hallway. Even though I heard him, I still dropped the keys out of my hands when he appeared in front of me.

"Why are you so jumpy?" He picks the keys up off the carpet and hands them to me.

Noah has been very supportive of my newfound career, but I'm not sure about how he is going to handle what I am about to tell him right now. We both knew that Tiffany wouldn't be gone forever, therefore what comes out of my mouth next shouldn't come as such a shock to him.

To be honest, I should have told him this already when we went to dinner last night and I know that.

Past Ellie wouldn't even bring it up at all, so I think I can give myself a little credit of my new behavior.

"She texted me." Sighing, I sit on the bed.

"What?" Noah's eyes widen as I expected. "You mean—"

"Yes. Her," I sigh. "She's actually texted me twice this week," I add.

"W--What?" Noah stammers. "You're just telling me about this?"

"She sent the first text message the other day when I was leaving therapy and then she texted me the next day when I was leaving the cemetery."

"You told Detective Carner about this, right?" He starts pacing around the bedroom.

"Well, no not yet. Noah--"

"Ellie…" More pacing.

"Just hear me out." I can tell my calmness is shocking my husband as he continues shaking his head and I remain seated on the bed.

"If I tell Detective Carner that Tiffany started contacting me, then she is going to want a police escort outside our house again, along with squad cars all around this town and probably the surrounding towns too. And I don't believe that's such a great idea right now. The presence of law enforcement will cause a scene and Detective Carner already did that years ago which scared Tiffany away. We can't allow her to draw attention to that psycho bitch. Alerting Tiffany would cause her to leave town and hide out again. Then who knows when I'll hear from her or even be this close to catching her? Then I'll never make any progress in the case."

"Ellie, this is not your case to make progress on. It's not your job to catch her. You are not even working on it. The detective is." Noah finally stops pacing to sit on the bed. "What did she tell you in the texts?"

"Well, she said she saw me at the cemetery."

"Ellie, you can't just drive around town knowing a serial killer is watching you," Noah starts frantically scrolling on his phone.

"Well, I've kind of already been doing that for a couple of years now." I point out, gesturing to the walls around us. "This time, I just have proof that she's close by." I scrunch my forehead, attempting to look over Noah's shoulder at his phone. His thumb scrolls rapidly on his screen. "What are you doing?"

"I'm pulling the security camera app up. We should look through all of the footage from last week. What if she's been around our property when we're sleeping? Or when we're not home? How the hell did she know you were at the cemetery? She must have followed you from here to there."

"Yes, I already thought of that." I sigh. "Noah, please just trust me. I'm not calling the detective or the police yet. They're not trustworthy and you know it. Stop looking through the cameras. I've looked through them several times already. She hasn't been here, and you're literally home every day. You would have seen or heard her and like I said, I checked the cameras multiple times. She may have watched me leave from here but she hasn't actually been on our property."

"Ellie," Noah gasps. "You need to call Detective Carner and let her know about this. Tiffany found us. She knows where we live."

Shaking my head, I grab my keys and stand up from the bed. "I know but just trust me please. I'm working on a case right now. I need to be cautious for my clients. Remember, I told you that I had an odd feeling about the case and you literally told me to always go with my instincts? I'm going with my instincts and my instincts tell me to not tell Detective Carner or anyone besides you."

"Why do my words always backfire on me?" My husband grunts to himself.

"The timing of both situations is a bit ironic. Don't you think?" Crossing my arms, I smile.

"I agree but if Tiffany is responsible for your client's disappearance, how would she have known that his brother would reach out to you specifically for your services and not any of the other P.I.'s in this town?" Noah questions. "Unless your client is working with her."

"I already thought of that too, but that's pretty doubtful." I disagree, shaking my head because I cannot see how or why Ben would be a part of a plan with Tiffany. During the time I spent in schooling myself about how to properly spot a liar back when I was secretly watching Chloe, I have learned how to spot one quite confidently. Ben has not shown any qualities of lying in our meeting in person or during any of our conversations over the phone.

"I need to go on with my day and you need to do the same thing. I have a meeting with someone for lunch. She was supposedly my client's date the night he went missing. I need to get going. We prepared for when Tiffany would come back. You know that—" I am abruptly interrupted when suddenly, my husband begins walking around the bed over to his night stand. "Now what are you doing?"

He pulls open his drawer, then pulls out his gun with his nondominant arm. Handling it with the muzzle up to the ceiling, finger off the trigger, he passes by me to walk out of the bedroom.

"Noah! What are you doing? You shouldn't handle that with your left arm. You only trained to use it with your right." I follow him into the hallway with my purse. I don't have time for this. I have things to do today— important things pertaining to work which I need to focus on since this is only my fourth client. My concentration needs to remain on this case, regardless of

Tiffany's sudden return. I won't let her become in control of my life.

He walks into the kitchen and places his gun on the counter next to the sink with the muzzle facing the backsplash of the wall. "Well, I'm home all day today so I should be cautious. Keeping this thing in the bedroom won't help me if I need it. Like you said, we prepared in case she came back." He begins pulling down the blinds in the kitchen before going into the living room. He is acting like we prepared for war or the Zombie apocalypse by the way he is moving around the house. Although, I can't blame him.

During the time of my study to become a P.I, Noah and I took firearms training classes for our protection. With knowing that Tiffany is still on the run, and after receiving threatening text messages from her, we knew moving towns, shifting work schedules and careers, along with installing an alarm and camera system on our house wouldn't be enough peace of mind in us truly believing we were safe.

Simply knowing how to handle a gun allows us more comfort when it comes to our safety. Not that I want to use my gun willingly on anyone. I rather only use it out of self-defense and I am more than prepared to defend myself against Tiffany. Clearly, Noah is too. But he did not have a broken arm when we trained at the range which is why I am uneasy with him handling his gun right now. I trust my husband. I don't trust his nondominant arm, however.

Other than wanting to defend myself from Tiffany, I trained to carry a gun because of my career. During my investigations, I am putting my life in danger when I am searching for my clients especially when I follow a person or show up to their door or place of work, asking personal questions they might not want to answer. They could get defensive which means, I need to defend myself back.

I never know what any of the investigations I conduct will entail until I get there, like today. I have no idea what awaits me when I go to meet Vee for lunch. Whatever happens, I hope it will be an answer to where the hell Cameron is.

1 9

January 9th
11:50 a.m.

I thought I got past not thinking my actions all the way through before acting upon them, but clearly, posting a video to social media about being involved with a wanted serial killer was something I overlooked. Instead of a response from Tiffany, the detective or anyone else with anything useful in response to my video, a news reporter from one of the neighboring towns— Jonesville, called me just now. They requested that I do an interview, but I quickly declined and hopefully, that will be the last conversation with a reporter that I'll have.

The news and media are not the attention I want to attract or thought about attracting when I posted my video. Hints and helpful clues from the public and obviously, a response from Tiffany is more preferable.

When getting out of my truck in front of the pizzeria to meet Vee, Detective Carner surprises me with another phone call about the stolen red Toyota from Montana.

"This morning, highway patrol found the car abandoned on the side of the highway facing northbound out of Fairview. There were no signs or traces of the person who stole the vehicle," she tells me, so I thank her for the update as I walk into the diner to meet Vee. There is no sense in asking the detective for any further information about the vehicle because I already know there isn't any.

Since the vehicle was ditched on the side of the highway, that tells me Tiffany really did learn to stop underestimating me. She must have known that I would go to the gas station to look at the surveillance footage and notice the stolen vehicle on camera after she texted me. She wanted me to see that she was nearby before getting rid of the vehicle so she wouldn't be tracked down.

But if she knew not to undervalue my investigative skills, then wouldn't she think I would report her to the police when she told me she was nearby?

Actually, no she wouldn't...

Because just like I have trained myself to get into her head, she's learned to get into mine. She not only relates to my anger; she also knows I won't trust the police to find her.

A notification from my phone alerts me that it is ten minutes until noon— the time I planned to meet Vee for lunch. Before I take a seat in a booth, I look around the restaurant at all of the customers. Eleven tables are taken. Six of the customers are women. I study each woman's facial features in the restaurant that could give a slight resemblance to the same complexion as Vee or

Tiffany. None of them merely resemble a match to either woman.

The bitch is a known serial killer but she is also a chameleon. Until I saw the wigs, the makeup, and the outfits in her house with Chloe, I hadn't realized how easy it was for a woman to simply become another woman. With a lot of effort, it isn't very hard to do. The irony.

Fifteen minutes after sitting at a booth in the pizzeria alone, it seems like Vee is running late, so I send her a message through Cameron's profile.

C: Just got here. Sitting in a booth on the right side.

Twenty minutes pass and still no response when I declare this a dead end. I did not want to result in ambushing the woman at her job but since she wants to stand me up, that is my next and only option.

2 0

January 9th
5:00 p.m.

Besides the unwanted call from a reporter earlier, nobody else has contacted me and I've only received eleven more reactions on my video. They say, if you want to get attention; the best way to do it is through social media. However, I disagree, especially if you have an almost non-existent presence like I do.

I walk into the grocery store where Vee works and grab a handheld basket. Out of the three cashiers, I spot her ringing up a customer's groceries.

I take a few minutes to walk around the aisles and grab three items that I don't really need.

When the customer walks off after paying, I put my items on the conveyor belt.

"Find everything alright?" She smiles.

"I did," I respond and hesitate before inserting my credit card into the machine as she scans the last item. "Excuse me, may I ask you a question?"

"What can I help you with?" She nods.

"Do you know this man?" Before completing the

transaction for my items, I show her an enlarged photo of Cameron on my phone screen.

Vee looks at my phone and scrunches her forehead. "Oh, uh… yes. Well, I don't know him that well, but we've met. We went out on a date a few nights ago. Why are you asking?"

"Was that the last time you saw or spoke to him?" I ask.

"I'm sorry, ma'am. What is this regarding?" Vee crosses her arms defensively, and rightfully so, since I have not introduced myself yet.

"My name is Ellie Moore. I am a local private investigator. Cameron Robinson has been missing for a few days now and I am currently searching for him. I understand you two went out on a date on the night of the fifth, the night he disappeared."

"Disappeared?" She repeats, uncrossing her arms, eyebrows raised. "But he messaged me last night to go on a second date. We were supposed to meet for lunch this afternoon except I kind of, well… I stood him up."

"When was the last time you saw him?"

"The night of our date. It was the fifth. He dropped me off after dinner. I hadn't heard from him until last night when he asked to meet for a lunch date today."

"When he dropped you off at home, did he go inside your house? Did you invite him in?" I question her.

Vee shakes her head, then nods to a customer who just put their items on the conveyor belt behind me. She directs her attention back to me. "He walked me to my door but I didn't invite him inside my house. He was respectful about it. I just didn't think we clicked that night."

"Then why did you agree to meet with him for lunch today?" I finish my transaction for my items and observe her mannerisms.

Two key traits to look out for when detecting if a person is lying are body movement and eye contact. Liars shift their bodies. They hesitate and avoid eye contact. They come up with lies to cover more lies. Good liars have endless lies planned up their sleeves. Bad liars stutter and do not have a good lie planned. This woman is not shifting her body or stuttering her words. She's looking right at me, stunned and confused.

"Well, I said yes to lunch because I thought about giving him another chance after our first date… but then I thought about it and really, I didn't have a great time with him. A lunch date didn't seem like it would make a difference. He was a nice guy but like I said, we didn't click. I was going to message him later and apologize for not showing up today."

Out of everything she said, the only lie out of her mouth is her last sentence. I surmise standing me up today wasn't the first time she has done that to someone before. I want to tell her simple communication goes a long way but I refrain from doing so. She also doesn't realize she stood me up today instead of Cameron.

As she begins ringing up the groceries for the customer behind me, I step off to the side near the carousel of grocery bags. "Just a few more questions before I go. On your way home from dinner, did anything unusual happen on the road while Cameron was driving? Any traffic incidents such as another driver cutting him off? Did he show off any road rage or encounter road rage from another driver? Did you happen to spot anyone tailing him?"

"No. The ride home was fine. I think we drove by only a couple cars but nobody cut him off while he was driving," she answers.

"Did you see Cameron drive away after he dropped you off?"

"Yes. I watched him drive away as I was turning to close the door when I walked in my house."

Since Cameron dropped Vee off at home, then my next stop is there.

"May I have your address, please? I need to drive the route from your house to Cameron's apartment so I can try to track down what happened to him after he left your house."

I do not need to ask Vee's permission for her address because I can find it on my own easily. But asking her will just simply save me time in searching for it when I get back in my truck. This way, I can head straight there from the grocery store.

Hesitantly, she shrugs. "Well…"

Before she attempts to tell me no, I politely remind her who I am and how I already found her here at work. Obtaining her legal address is not out of formality for me. I'm asking out of courtesy because it will help in speeding up my efforts in finding Cameron— the nice man she feels bad about standing up for lunch today.

After successfully guilt tripping her – a tactic I have no shame in doing when it comes to finding my client, Vee gives in. Her house is only an eight-minute drive from here. Before I am about to leave, she looks at me with confusion. "How did Cameron message me last night if he's been missing since the last time that I saw him? Do you think someone else was messaging me?"

"I'm not sure yet, but thank you for your cooperation."

"This is crazy. I hope you find him. He seemed like a good guy but after meeting him, he just wasn't my type. You know?" She shakes her head.

Nodding, I agree even though I don't relate at all because I have been married to Noah for a decade. I can't and do not want to remember what dating is like before we met each other.

Before pulling out of the parking spot at the grocery store, I direct myself to Vee's address. After Cameron dropped her off, he should have gone straight home unless he decided to stop somewhere along the way. Maybe a convenience store for more cigarettes or possibly, he needed to fill up for gas?

About eight minutes later, I take a left onto Flagler Street where Vee resides. Then I re-direct myself on the map to Thornberry Street where Cameron and Ben's apartment is. There are three route options from Vee's house to their apartment. Each route says it takes about a ten-to-twelve-minute drive.

Route A: A left off Flagler Street. Then a right at the third stop sign, turning onto Seely Street. And then a left onto Thornberry Street.

Route B: A left off Flagler Street. Then a right at the second stop sign, two hundred feet down, turning onto Johnson Ave. Then a left onto Thornberry Street.

Route C: A left off Flager Street. Then a right at the first stop sign that's a hundred feet down, turning onto Wheeler Rd which extends for almost two miles. Then a left at the next light on Thornberry Street.

Beginning with Route A, I leave Vee's house and turn left onto Flagler Street, keeping my eyes open for any sign of Cameron or his truck along the way.

2 1

January 9th
5:30 p.m.

Route A takes me through a small neighborhood where the houses are about five hundred feet apart from each other. There is one gas station on Seely Street. A security camera is mounted outside of the entrance so I stopped in and asked the attendant to see his surveillance footage on the fifth. Unfortunately, my timing of arrival did not work out in my favor because the teenage cashier could not access the cameras without the owner (her mother) even if she tried. She told me to come back when the owner arrives which should be in an hour. I continued on my way and completed the route to Cameron and Ben's apartment.

I just arrived outside. I stopped into the corner store a block over from their apartment and looked at the footage from that night. The last time Cameron was seen on camera was at 7:32 p.m., the time of his last transaction. No sign of Cameron or his vehicle along the way either.

From their apartment, I select the Route B option

to direct myself back to Vee's house. This route takes me through part of the same neighborhood as the first route did. Except there are no gas stations to stop in along the way. No evidence of Cameron or his truck along this route either.

I arrive at Vee's house again and from here, I direct myself back to Ben and Cameron's apartment one last time. This road takes me through part of the same neighborhood again, until it turns into a road that parallels dense woods. Once the woods come into my view, I find myself more hopeful and a bit frustrated that I didn't think to drive down this route first. If something suspicious or out of the ordinary were to happen in this town, the chances are likely to happen out in these woods especially at night without any streetlights on the road.

For about two miles, this road stretches alongside the woods without any houses or businesses in sight until I reach Thornberry Street.

Driving slowly while taking advantage of the empty road behind me, my eyes scan for any abnormalities off the side of the road and near the woods such as clothing, and damaged vehicle parts like benders, hub caps, or tires. I especially look out for broken parts from a truck, which I would take notice of because I own one myself.

Even if it seems like nothing, anything is always worth looking into.

A half-mile further, skid marks in the pavement on the right side of the road catch my eye. I pull over and observe the direction of the tracks. The tire marks appear to have veered onto the grass, then back onto the shoulder— as if the vehicle skidded off the road for a moment before regaining control again. I surmise the vehicle had to swerve out of the way of something, such as another vehicle to avoid an accident. Although the possibilities of an accident happening on this road with the next to nothing traffic seems slim. Not impossible, however.

I continue driving another half mile down. Something blue sticks out of the grass just a few feet amongst the tree line on the same side of the road where I just passed the skid marks. As I pull my truck over to park in the grass, I see that it's a net…a pool cleaning net. Three bottles of chlorine tablets for swimming pools lay in the dirt only a few feet next to it.

Ben told me, one of Cameron's jobs as a handyman consists of cleaning pools… And the skid marks alongside the road look large enough to come from wheels belonging to a truck.

I get out of the driver's side and walk into the woods toward the cleaning supplies. There is no company name or anything identifying the supplies belong to Cameron. Leaving the supplies on the ground, I set off to explore farther past the tree line of the forest. I can't say, this is the first time my theories left me on an impromptu trek through the woods without a plan. But at least this time, I am following a physical clue and I can take comfort in knowing that I am armed to defend myself. I've also become more self-aware since then.

The route to Cameron's house, the pool supplies, and the tire tracks cannot be a coincidence.

A hundred yards into the woods, I do not see any more pool cleaning supplies or anything else alarming…

until something metallic sticks out in the dirt ahead of me.

When switching my pace from a walk to a jog toward the object, I realize it's a money clip wallet.

Cameron Robinson's license and his insurance card is inside, but everything else is gone. No credit cards, debit cards, or cash. It looks like he was robbed.

Thieves normally empty the contents of their victim's wallets and only take what is valuable. They usually disregard the persons driver's license and anything else that is not valuable or could be incriminating to take. Better to leave the identity of the victim at the scene of the crime instead of having it on you.

I presume somebody must have driven Cameron off the road as I first suspected when seeing the tracks. But I don't believe it was to avoid an accident. I think, someone targeted him on purpose.

But what would make a person drive Cameron off the road and into the woods only for a wallet and a truck? A classic case of road rage does not normally involve robbing someone and chasing them out of their vehicle…

The direction of the skid marks on the road tells me the thief drove away with his truck once Cameron exited the vehicle. I do not see any footprints in the ground near the spot where I found his wallet. Then again, there shouldn't be any because Cameron has been missing for days now and it's rained at least once every day since then. Any footprints or tracks in the dirt would be washed away by now.

If the wallet was closer to the pool supplies at the

beginning of the woods, I would believe that the thief chucked it into the woods after stealing what he needed. Except, my analysis of the scene tells me that is not the case. Right here where I stand, was a point of altercation. So then where did Cameron go from here?

"Cameron!" I shout, hoping to hear some form of a response. "Cameron!"

The sound of the trees rustling in the wind surrounds me. I call his name several more times, louder each time.

The wind and the trees only answer me. There are more than a hundred acres of these woods. About three miles ahead of me deeper into these woods, there are freshwater springs which is closed off to the public for the season. My house is about a ten-minute drive further down the road to the west from here. If I were to keep trekking farther into the woods, I would likely end up in my front yard at one point.

It will take way too much time for me to hike all this land on my own, but I need to rule out the possibility that Cameron could be out here in these woods somewhere.

On my way back to my truck, I make a call to Fairview's police department. This is the first time I am requesting search team assistance from law enforcement as a private investigator but my request should not be denied. Between finding Cameron's license, the pool equipment, along with the direction of the skid marks on the road, and a record of Ben attempting to file a missing person's report days ago, there is enough probable cause to get a search team out here.

2 2

Instead of tampering with the scene, I took a few photos and videos of Cameron's wallet and of the pool supplies in the woods before going to the police station.

An unnecessarily long hour and a half after requesting for a search team, five Fairview police officers finally came out and searched the area.

The search team is divided into teams of two out of a group of ten people, not counting Ben and I who are teamed up together. As I've said before, I like to keep my clients updated— whether it is bad, good, or uncertain.

About fifteen minutes into the search just after the sun has fully set, I am starting to wonder if I made a bad decision in choosing to utilize the expenses of law enforcement. But then a call for an airlift comes across the radio from another search member who is near the springs.

"Holy shit! They found him?" Ben gasps.

"Sounds like someone found something... Let's

go back to the base."

Minutes later, we arrive back to where the search began and I find an officer.

"Did someone find my brother?" Ben frantically asks.

"We did but we're not sure what condition he's in yet. The airlift is on the way. I suggest going to the hospital to meet him there."

Ben looks at me with a loss of words. In panic, it becomes hard to think straight, so I do it for him. "Leave your car here. You'll ride with me. By the time the airlift gets to the hospital, we'll already be there waiting," I say.

Ben agrees with me and we head to my truck. "You don't think he's… he's dead, do you?" He stammers.

"They wouldn't have called in an airlift for a dead body." I shake my head, trying to reassure him.

What I just said is true, yet that doesn't mean whatever condition Cameron might be in isn't critical.

Twenty minutes later, Ben and I arrive at the hospital and I use my I.D. to get us through the emergency room. Shortly after, a nurse notifies me that the airlift just arrived.

Hooked up to an oxygen I.V. with bruises all over his head and dried blood stuck to his neck, Cameron is awake but barely coherent as paramedics rush him into the ER.

"Both of his legs are broken and he is severely malnourished." A paramedic tells an ER nurse as they wheel him through the halls. Ben and I rush behind them closely.

"What happened?" Ben asks to the paramedic wheeling him in. "He said three men tailgated him on his way home from a date a few days ago. They drove him off the road before crashing into the back of his truck. He said the men got out and surrounded his vehicle, then pulled him out of the driver's side. He fought them off and took off running into the woods. The thieves went after him, beat him up, and took off."

"They wanted my truck," Cameron interrupts while holding the oxygen mask away from his mouth to speak. "Followed me from the stop sign," he wheezes and puts the oxygen mask back on for a moment. "They f—fucking beat my legs with crowbars. I crawled to the springs f—for water."

To think, if it weren't for the small freshwater springs a few acres into the woods, the paramedics would be carrying Cameron out in a body bag instead of into the emergency room. If this had happened during the season, someone would have seen Cameron long before I went out there to look for him.

We are approaching the doors in the ER that none of us are allowed to go through besides the hospital staff.

What I am about to do is very out of protocol and equally inappropriate timing but I pull out my phone to show Cameron a photo of Tiffany. It is important that I ask him about her now before he undergoes surgery. The longer I wait, the longer Tiffany remains on the run, and honestly, I'm too impatient. He said he was robbed by men, but Tiffany could have been in the truck or apart of the robbing too. "Before you go, do you know this woman?"

"Avery's serial killer." Cameron groggily answers, exchanging a confused glance from my phone to Ben.

"This is Ellie. She's a private investigator. I hired her to look for you," Ben explains and the look on Cameron's face turns into more confusion.

"Was she with the group of men who ran you off the road?" I ask Cameron, and he shakes his head.

"We need to take him back now. I'm sorry. You will have to continue your questions later." One of the nurses sternly tells me. I apologize and allow the staff to do their jobs.

"Let's go find an officer," I tell Ben, gesturing toward the waiting room where I spot an officer from the search team.

"Sir, your bother was in an altercation and a victim to tailgating."

"Yes, the paramedic just explained that to us," Ben hastily answers.

"When he is able to, I will need to talk to him and see if he can ID the perpetrators when he comes out of surgery. The department has received similar reports of road rage and robberies to other victims in the area as well. I need to get his statement as soon as possible."

"Do you have any suspects yet?" I ask.

"We have a group of males in mind." The officer nods.

"But no women at all?"

"No, ma'am."

Since this officer is adamant that a woman is not a part of my client's mugging and carjacking, now I can focus my full attention on locating Tiffany.

Now my new client is her. However, contrary to my usual objective when solving investigations, my aim is not to find her safely this time.

2 3

TIFFANY

Another man saved by Ellie. How endearing of her. Watching Ben sleep in a chair besides his broken brother who is also sound asleep looks sentimental to anyone else but me. I could open this hospital room door all the way, walk right in without anyone noticing, and smash both Cameron and Ben over the back of their heads.

Ben first because he's in the chair closest to the door. Then Cameron because he's basically paralyzed with two broken legs and drugged up in the bed. They would both be dead before a nurse walked in and I'd be gone before anyone saw me. Except, I have to fight the urge of how easy it is to kill them tonight because even though there are only three nurses on this floor, three people around are too much of a risk for me to act upon my desires.

Ellie should take a lesson from me when it comes to resisting upon acting on her intrusive thoughts and theories.

Regardless of the few nurses on staff tonight, I did not come here with the intention of killing Ben and Cameron. I came here so Ellie will know how close I can get to her.

"Do you need assistance?" Speaking of nurses, a woman wearing black scrubs with yellow colored cartoon cats on it, smiles innocently at me in the hallway.

I pull my hat down lower to cover my eyes and forehead, and silently close the door to Cameron's room. "No, thank you. I'll come back when they are awake tomorrow."

The nurse smiles and walks away, unsuspecting of me as she should be.

24

January 11th
5:05 a.m.

Two days have gone by since Cameron was found. I thought he and Ben were safe from Tiffany Burnes since Cameron has been in the hospital since then, but I was wrong.

Two hours ago, I received four text messages that I didn't see it until I just woke up a moment ago.

Beginning with a photo, the first message is the most daunting— Cameron is sleeping in the hospital with casts around both of his legs. An IV is hooked up to his arm, while Ben sleeps on a visitor chair beside him. By the angle of the way the photo was taken, it is clear Tiffany clandestinely was standing outside of the door when she took it.

Three text messages follow the photo.

Your video won't help you at all, Ellie.

And good job at solving your recent case. After saving Cameron, it would be a shame if

something tragic were to happen to him.

Or to his brother, Ben.

My video prompted a response out of her, yet this isn't the type of response I wanted. I brought my client back to his family safely and at the same time, I ended up putting him in danger. Knowing there is no use, I call the number from the text while rushing out of bed, then down the hallway to my office.

"The number you dialed is not in service."

I input the phone number into a geolocation search on my computer and call Ben.

After a couple of rings, his voicemail comes back on the other end.

Fuck.

I hang up and call Cameron's phone number, pacing behind my desk impatiently until he answers.

The area code on the phone number from this message is the same area code the second text message came from; Jacksonville. There is no way Tiffany is in that city right now because she just proved she was in the hospital only two hours ago by sending the photo of Cameron and Ben. Jacksonville is a six-hour drive from Fairview…

Tiffany's still in the area.

Hopefully, not still in the hospital…

Relief floods over me when Cameron finally answers my call in a groggy whisper.

"Hi, Cameron. Sorry to wake you. This is private investigator, Ellie Moore. I'm not sure if you remember meeting me in the hospital."

"Yes. I slightly do," Cameron answers.

"I was just calling to check in and see how you're doing. Is Ben with you?"

"Yes, he's sleeping. I think the doctor's releasing me later today."

I'm not sure if releasing Cameron so soon is a good or bad thing. Tiffany was already outside of his hospital room, meaning it wouldn't be difficult for her to get to them in their own home either. Then again, if she had intentions to harm them, she would have done so already…

Instead of letting Cameron know that Tiffany was only just a few feet away from him while he was asleep, I decide to explain why I'm calling in lighter terms. No sense in alarming the man when he's literally stuck in bed. "I do not want to frighten you, but I was also calling for another reason. I am not sure if your brother explained anything about my involvement in the Tiffany Burnes case to you yet."

"Mhm," Cameron mumbles. "He mentioned something to me. You asked me bout' her before, didn't you?"

"Yes, I did. Well, I have reason to believe that she's returned to Avery and I would like everyone who is associated with me to be aware. I have yet to inform the police because I am not working with them on her case, and I'd like to keep it that way for now. Of course, you have the option to call the police department with this information because it is not my place to tell you what to do. Legally, if you feel unsafe, you have every right to let them know what I just told you. I just wanted to make you aware of the situation because my job is to keep you safe."

"You've already brought be to safety," Cameron says. "You're the reason I'm alive."

"And my intentions are to keep it that way."

Thankfully as I expected and hoped for, since the police did not list Cameron as missing, he assures me that his trust falls all with me, rather than with law enforcement. He promised to keep what I just told him to himself and Ben who he will fill in when he wakes up. He doesn't ask me any more questions about my involvement and I believe it's because he is too drained from his own traumatic experience. I encouraged him to be conscious of his surroundings and when it comes to meeting new women once he makes a full recovery, get to know who they are before being anywhere alone with them. Even though he has seen Tiffany's picture, he cannot underestimate her skills of being a chameleon. Nobody can.

Before getting off the phone, I let him know to call me if he or Ben encounter anything strange in the next few days. No matter the time of day or night.

As I look at the photo of Ben and Cameron on the message, I speculate why Tiffany chose to threaten them and not act upon any malicious intent while she was there. Tiffany hates how I advocate for males and that I brought justice to her families of her victims. And above all, she had a hatred for men long before she met me.

That same hatred for males has been carried over to me.

Other than Noah who is nearly impossible for her to get to, and my father who lives several states away and hasn't contacted me in over a year, there is no other man significant in my life to threaten besides Ben and Cameron. Tiffany wants me to live in fear; to not only worry about myself, but the people around me. Right now, those people are my clients. I believe the photo was sent as more of proof, less so than a threat. Her purpose was to prove she's still around— To tell me nothing is stopping her from going unnoticed.

Keeping my promise of not keeping secrets from my husband, I already woke Noah up and showed him the messages.

He brings in a cup of coffee for me while I think aloud and stare at my *Tiffany Burnes* board.

"I wonder how Jake's doing," I murmur when looking at his photo. Next to his name, the words, RESCUED BY ME & CHLOE are written.

Jake would have been another one of her victims if it hadn't been for Chloe and I. When we saw Tiffany leave the house alone without him, we took the opportunity to break through the back door and inadvertently saved him from getting bludgeoned and axed to death in her attic. If Tiffany didn't underestimate Chloe and I that night, all three of us would have been dead and buried in her backyard.

I spoke to Jake a few days after Chloe was murdered. He knows why Tiffany claimed Chloe as her ninth victim but Detective Carner instructed him to keep that information and my involvement in the case to himself. Just like she instructed me to keep my mouth shut, *'for our safety.'*

As far as I know, he hasn't told anyone the real story. When I checked on his social media last month, he seemed to be doing fine and has kept my name offline. He's briefly mentioned that he was almost a victim of Tiffany if it hadn't been for the police arriving to her house that night, but as for mentioning mine and Chloe's names, I haven't seen either anywhere on his profiles. From his persona, I trust he remains true to his word.

"You haven't spoken to him lately?" Noah places the cups on my desk.

"No. Not since Chloe died. I don't think I really need to reach out to him though. I'm just wondering how he's been."

"Well, Tiffany is back in town so don't you think she would target Jake again? Don't you think she's probably mad that she didn't finish what she started before? Maybe you should reach out to him."

I understand what my husband is saying. He thinks Tiffany wants to come back and finish the job with Jake because I stopped her before. But Noah is not thinking like Tiffany does. Her vendetta is not with Jake. It's with me.

My eyes skim across the board to the text message where she confessed to mistakenly underestimating Chloe and I the night we rescued Jake.

I didn't have enough supplies to drug all three of you. When I left Jake in the attic, I planned to come back and finish the job. But I underestimated you and Chloe.

If we never broke-in while Tiffany was gone and instead knocked on her door when she was home, she would have tried to invite us in for drinks where she had plans to inexplicably drug us to unconsciousness.

If it weren't for Tiffany, then I wouldn't be in the situation that I'm in now. Just like Tiffany wouldn't be in the situation that she's in now if it weren't for me.

I am glad that I didn't fall victim to her crime that night, yet I am still upset about my uprooted life. I know she feels the same way. I can understand her anger but the thing is, she does not understand mine. Not after she killed Chloe.

"You make a good point but I don't believe Jake will be a target of hers again because he was already her victim. Jake didn't get away from her on his own freewill. If he did, maybe you would be right but he got away because of me. She already killed Chloe. Now she only cares about getting back at me."

"Then why hasn't she tried to kill you or your clients yet? What's the point in texting you their photo if you think she won't hurt them? Why would she be so bold to show you that she was next to them and not do anything." Noah shakes his head, staring at the board. "Not that I want her to kill anyone. None of this makes sense. Are we even sure that it's her texting you? Maybe it's someone trying to play a sick prank."

"It's her, Noah. I know it is," I insist. "Tiffany hasn't tried to harm me or you because she's had plenty of time to try by now. Her motive is revenge and the best form of revenge is to make a person suffer. It's fear. That's why she's texting me without a way for me to respond. She's in control of the situation. She wants me to fear that my clients are in danger now and that's why she sent me their photo. Except I don't think they actually are."

"That's why you the investigator, and I'm not." Noah smirks. "You sure it's not time to call the detective yet? You don't want to put your clients in danger."

"Yes, I know that." I try to respond without a tone of disdain because Noah is right and understandably very worried about the situation. I know he is also frustrated with the fact that none of this is in his control and instead, all in mine. I got us into this mess and I promise to get us out of it.

Since Tiffany proclaimed she would keep tabs on me and learned so much about my life during the first time she contacted me, I've already assumed she knows my parents live in New York and Noah's parents live in Chicago. But I'm not sure if she knows that both of us have not had any contact with either of them in a year. We haven't even seen them in person in about four. Does she know that we both share strained relationships with our family? Another similarity that we bonded over besides not having any siblings.

Even though I do not believe Tiffany has any indication to go after mine or Noah's family because if she wanted them dead, she's had plenty of time to kill them by now, I still decide to make a painful suggestion. "We should call our parents."

"After not talking to them in over a year, we're going to call and let them know a serial killer's been after us for even longer?" Noah huffs a sarcastic laugh.

"I think my mom's going to be more furious that we didn't tell her we moved instead." I shrug.

He hands me my phone. "I'll make my call when you make yours."

2 5

After I get home from group therapy which admittedly was needed today, Noah and I are going to give our parents a call again since neither his or mine answered this morning. Until then, Noah desperately wants me to call Detective Carner but if I do, not much will get done quickly. Yes, Tiffany is one of the most relevant and prolific killers with an open investigation in America at the moment. However, telling Detective Carner about the new messages would not only prompt her to plant a police escort outside of my house, but in turn, a hindrance in my own investigation. And drawing attention to Tiffany is not what I want right now.

Between receiving the text messages, solving Cameron's case and my last visit at the cemetery, I admit that I actually looked forward to attending a therapy session for the first time today. Although I opted to stay silent when it hit my turn to share in the group since I shared last week, hearing everyone else talk about what's going on in their lives distracted me from my own thoughts.

At least it did for the time being. I am trying to leave the room before Emma catches me at the door, but I am too late.

"You want to get lunch or do you have to work on a secret case you can't tell me about?" She crosses her arms, smiling.

It really isn't fair to Emma if I keep avoiding her. We've only had lunch twice outside of therapy which turned out great and it'd be nice to go out again. Just not right now when Tiffany has proven she's nearby and watching me. There is no way my second new friend is going to end up dead because of me. "I can't today but follow me to my truck."

We head out of the building to the parking lot. My eyes scan our surroundings cautiously.

"Why do you look so paranoid?" Emma whispers.

When we get in my truck, I lock the doors and look in the backseat.

All clear.

In the passenger seat, Emma turns around to follow my gaze behind us. "You alright?" She scrunches her forehead.

"I'm fine. Well, kind of. I can't be seen out in public with you right now." I turn around to face the steering wheel, keeping my eyesight on the parking lot. There are only six cars here and all of them belong to the members in our grief group. Since it's the weekend, the three other businesses who share this plaza with the therapy group are closed. Two members are getting in a truck together. Another member is already backing his

SUV out of a parking spot. The last two people from our group are getting ready to back their cars out too. Besides Emma's blue car, the last vehicle parked in the lot belongs to Dr. Bennett, who is walking out of the building now.

"What's going on with you?" Emma asks, concern written over her face. "Just tell me. You know I won't take offense to anything."

"I know you won't. This has nothing to do with you." I shake my head, sighing. "As you know, I'm the reason Jamie died."

"You're not the reason." Emma places a hand on my arm. "Just because you were across the street when she was murdered, doesn't mean you were the reason for her death. There's no way you could have known what was going on. You need to stop blaming yourself for not being there for her. I know, I'm one to talk."

If Emma knew the real story, I am certain she would agree with me instead. It would be nice to be truthful with her and feel what it's like to confide in a friend again; another female who I can trust and let my guard down around. Except the outcome of my only and last two friendships haven't allowed me to do so yet.

"I haven't told you this but I actually had a big involvement in the Tiffany Burnes case. I still kind of do. I was the person who brought her to the police's attention in Avery. It's a very long story and I can't tell you all the details but I might not be safe from her right now. Tiffany knows who I am and as you can imagine, she's not too happy with me." I break my sight from the windshield to look at Emma.

"Oh, wow! So you figured out who Tiffany was?

How?"

"I—I can't really go into detail about that with you yet."

When Tifffany is finally behind bars, or better yet dead, I will tell Emma the full story. Until then, she is just going to have to keep her questions to herself.

"I understand." Emma looks out of her window, then brings her attention back on me. "So, is that why you're paying attention to everything around us right now? Do you think she's watching us?"

"Uh, possibly. I believe she is in town and if we're seen together anywhere in public, I'm worried she will see us and I don't want her to target you because she's trying to get to me," I hesitate. "I just didn't want you to think that I am avoiding you. I mean, I *am* avoiding you, just not for a bad reason."

Emma laughs. "I understand. We'll lay low for a bit. But if you need me, you know I'm here for you. I had no idea you were a part of that case. Wow! I have a lot of questions when you're ready to answer them."

"Oh, I bet you do!" I huff a laugh. "I'm going to watch you walk to your car now and then I'll follow you out to the streetlight. Make sure you check your mirrors often on your drive home. Pay attention to the vehicles behind you. Make sure no one tries to follow you and call me if you suspect anything or anyone odd around you. Just please, stay vigilant—" I stop continuing to make an ass out of myself and shut my mouth.

I should not even imply to this woman that she doesn't know how to look out for herself. The murder of her sister led Emma to become more self-aware. She vowed to learn how to defend herself, reflecting on how she and her sister could have benefited from such awareness earlier.

In addition to guilt, death often triggers profound realizations. It's not until it's too late that we recognize the importance of certain actions, behavior, and being attentive.

Between working as a part-time nurse, Emma fills her week with a boxing class, a karate class, a self-defense course and she works out at the gym. I don't know how she does it, but it's impressive.

"Sorry. I shouldn't need to tell you how to defend yourself," I say.

"It's okay." Emma shrugs. "I appreciate how much you care about me even though you barely know me."

"You're the type of person who makes it hard not to care about." I smile. "But I know you can handle yourself."

"Which speaking of handling myself, I think now would be a great time to finally attend a class with me. My self-defense class is next Monday, if you want to join. We don't even have to meet outside the place. We can act like we never met. In case that bitch is watching you. You'll be able to let all your stress out in the class. I'm telling you, fighting is really good for you," Emma says before getting out of my truck.

These interactions with Emma remind me so much of Laura and a little bit of Chloe at times too.

"I promise when I feel that it's safe to be around me, I'll go to a class with you. Not sure it will be next Monday though." I smile, vowing to myself that I will keep my promise and act upon it when Tiffany is finally out of my life.

The psycho bitch took one friend away from me. There is no way that I'll allow her to take another.

2 6

On my computer, I watch a video of a reporter from Brookesview news station.

"Forty-year-old, Jesse Jameson was found bludgeoned to death in this motel 8 behind me here in Brookesview early this morning. Authorities speculate the victim had been in the hotel for at least a day before his body was found by the hotel housemaid. With the two-year anniversary just passing since Tiffany Burne's claimed her last victim, and her last known crimes taken place just an hour outside of our own hometown, residents of Brookesview can't help but wonder, has she returned? Or is the timing coincidental? With only one homicide here in Brookesview a year, and Tiffany's previous crimes in our neighboring town, what are the chances?"

Brookesview is another small town an hour north of Fairview and an hour south of Avery. I have never met the victim, so if Tiffany was behind his murder, what made her target him?

I called Ben and asked whether he or his brother has any connections to Jesse. He told me, they both never met or heard of him before. Noah doesn't know who Jesse is and Emma texted me back after I sent her the news link a few minutes ago, saying she does not know him either.

The closest people around me have no connection to Jesse, so then why would Tiffany choose to kill him? The speculation of her being responsible for this murder is probably just the media spreading a story that isn't true.

Then again with my knowledge of Tiffany nearby, in hindsight the medias story might not be so implausible. Maybe his death wasn't planned. Maybe his death was the cause of an accidental slip up on her part.

While making a call to Detective Carner, I stare out at the woods outside of my office window. Overcast skies are beginning to cover the sunrise, warning a morning thunderstorm is about to roll in.

"I'm guessing you heard about Jesse Jameson?" Detective Carner greets me over the phone.

"I did. Is it true? Did Tiffany kill that man?" I walk away from my window to print the news report off my computer.

"When I receive the results of the autopsy report, then I'll know more. It won't be another few days, maybe a week until the results come back," Detective Carner says.

Opposed to being a single male in his twenties or early thirties which is Tiffany's prime target, the news report said Jesse was forty years old and married.

"Jesse doesn't fit her usual targeted victim's profile though." I remove the news article from my printer under my desk and tack it onto my board, highlighting the date of his death.

Detective Carner sighs. "She could be creating a different pattern. Maybe Tiffany's starting a new victim list and Jesse was just added to it. We don't know what she's been doing these past few years. She could be killing in a new pattern or maybe not even killing at all."

But don't you think you should know the answer to those questions though? If the police can't find her, am I the only one who will?

I shift my attention from the news article to the *'murder weapon?'* note on my board. "If she is responsible for his death, are you going to let the public know about the details of the murder weapon now?"

"If the autopsy confirms the indentation in Jesse's skull as the same one on her previous victims, then yes. I will need to inform the public about the weapon. You know that I've been concerned with copycat killers emerging which is why I didn't want the weapon to be public knowledge. I don't need any copycat killers to throw off the investigation."

"But how many people would be able to copycat Tiffany with the same weapon when you don't even know what the weapon is yet?" Dead air fills the phone line. I am starting to irritate her which causes me to push her buttons even more. "Unless you *do* know what the weapon is and you can't tell me."

"No. I do not know, Ellie." Detective Carner responds.

When the victims were found buried in Tiffany's

backyard, the autopsy reports ended up revealing a two-inch wide indentation in the shape of a heart on the back of their skulls. Investigators determined whatever object was used needed to be heavy enough to bludgeon the victims, resulting to their final deaths. Besides law enforcement who are working on the case, I believe that I am the only person who has been informed with the details of Tiffany's murder weapon, specifically the size and shape.

Detective Carner told me about it in the beginning of the investigation when I was technically unofficially a part of it. Since then, she has been honest with me about Tiffany Burnes to the extent of my knowledge, but because I am not officially a part of the case and never have been, I sense there are more details being held from me. I am fully aware that legally, she can't divulge every piece of new information to me. But when it comes to the murder weapon, she must have some sort of a clue as to what it is by now.

"Did you talk to Jesse's wife?" I ask because the murder happened in a town outside of Avery; the detectives jurisdiction. Yet with speculation surrounding Tiffany, Detective Carner might be working on his investigation too.

"Jesse told his wife that he would be home late the other night after getting drinks with some co-workers but nobody that's been questioned so far, can attest to going out with him or making any plans together that night."

"You mean, his wife never called to report her husband missing?" I question.

If Noah didn't come home, I'd call and text him

nonstop and if he didn't answer, I would head straight to the police station to report him missing. Then I would start searching for him myself. Just like he did when he ran into Avery's police station to report me missing because I wasn't answering his calls and text messages.

"His wife said they got in an argument which is why he went out for drinks after work. Apparently, it was not out of the ordinary for him to leave for a day or a couple days after an argument between them."

I thank Detective Carner for the information before ending the call, opting out in letting her know about the recent messages between Tiffany and I. Or should I say *from Tiffany* since there is no way for me to text her back.

"Ellie, before we hang up. I want to remind you that you are not part of this case. I saw your video. I know very well that I cannot stop you from conducting your own investigation, but please be careful and call me with any valuable information you might receive."

When we get off the phone, I decide to do another search for the murder weapon. Until my conversation with the detective just now, the weapon has not been in the forefront of my mind.

Before Chloe died, I tried searching online for something in the shape of a small heart that could be remotely capable for murder. I never found anything promising. But I didn't really dive deep into the search.

Even if I do find out what Tiffany's murder weapon is, what use will it be? It's not like the weapon could link me to Tiffany's whereabouts now.

Then again, since Jesse just came up dead, it won't hurt to pick up on the search once more. Whatever her choice of weapon is, the thing has to have more significance to Tiffany than we know. Or at least that Detective Carner is telling me.

A heart symbol is normally associated with love and affection. Did the weapon start out as a gift from a man who ended up being her first victim? A man who maybe, treated her wrong. A cheater, abuser, or just a shitty guy in general? What started as revenge ended up as a gruesome hobby. Does her twisted mind work that way or am I trying too hard to think like her?

Whatever led Tiffany to her first victim, I can't make myself see a justifiable reason for her actions at all.

In the search bar on my computer, I type the same phrase I have searched before: *Heart shaped objects for women.*

As I've become familiar with the first page results, nothing has changed from the list of baking utensils, cookie cutters, cooking pots and pans which are all made into a heart shape. Down the next page, I scroll past a few results showing sex toys, makeup and beauty products such as curling irons, face rollers, hair brushes, and concealer brushes. Each item has a form of a heart decoration, but nothing seems heavy enough to bludgeon a man.

Further down, I see more baking utensils, mirrors, computer mouses and mouse pads, and body massagers....

I am realizing that anything can be created into the shape of a heart to make it look more feminine, even the handles on a kitchen knife set. What is made for man these days, can be made for a woman. Or at least, can try to be.

On the next page of results, the list transforms to self-defense objects beginning with a pink taser and then pink mace. I carry both weapons myself except they are not pink and not heavy enough to bludgeon a person.

In the search bar, I type the phrase: *Heart shaped self-defense tools for women.*

The first result in the list shows a pair of heart-shaped brass knuckles. They could be heavy enough to knock a person out, but the placement of the knuckles are too close together. There was only one heart shaped indentation in the skulls of Tiffany's victims, so the brass knuckles can be ruled out as a possible option.

A pocket knife with a heart shaped handle is listed below the brass knuckles, then a silver pendant in the shape of a heart necklace that holds a self-defense alarm button. The necklace is designed to call the police, alerting them to your location when you press the button. Useful, but not for Tiffany.

Narrowing my options, I update the search phrase: *Heart shaped self-defense tools that are two inches wide.*

The first page shows me the same results as before.

Think like a killer. What would I use to kill a man if I had to?

If it were out of self-defense, my gun would be my first option but we know Tiffany isn't using one…

But I know she's used an axe before.

Besides the mysterious unknown object that is used to knock her victims out, she also utilized an axe to cut their bodies up before burying them in her backyard.

I saw the axe, a blood-dried knife, and a bunch of tools scattered on a table in her attic where Chloe and I found Jake. My attention remained focused on cutting him out of the ropes to get the hell out of there… but as I think back to that moment, I recall seeing pink plyers on the table.

I didn't think twice about the plyers until now.

As I have learned while conducting this search, *anything can be made to look feminine*. Add something pink or purple, a cute pattern like hearts around a kitchen knife set and suddenly, the object or product becomes more appeaseable to a female.

I update the search phrase to: *heart shaped constructing tools for women that are two inches wide*.

The first two results reveal a set of pink hammers and a red screwdriver set. Purple colored hearts decorate the handles of each tool. I scroll down the list, past a couple more brightly colored decorated tools. Some of these tools are toys, labelled for children.

On the second page, four listings down, a carbon steel single hole puncher with a heart stamp engraved on the end strikes my eye. The details for the product description says it's available in different sizes, from one to three inches wide.

Before I click on the listing, my eyes divert to another even likelier option below the puncher.

A pink toolbox which is decorated in red hearts contains a set of tools that are all colored pink as well: a wrench, plyers, a drill set and most importantly— a mallet hammer that has a small heart shape stamp engraved on the face of it. The product details do not tell me the size of the stamp, but it looks to be at least an inch or two inches wide from the customer review photos.

RONA'S FEMININE TOOLS sells the single steel hole puncher and the toolbox. They are just listed as separate items. The store makes custom items such as stationary, crafting tools, and toolbox sets for women. It says the shop is online and has been in business for over twelve years.

I am disappointed in myself that I did not dive deeper when I first looked into this years ago. Especially when it just took me only about twenty minutes to find these tools. So then if I just stumbled upon these results this easily, the detective should know this too, right?

I add the toolbox and the steel hole puncher to the cart on the website and hit checkout.

With expedited shipping, both items should be delivered to my house by tomorrow evening.

2 7

January 12th
8:30 p.m.

"Are you sure you're ready to do this?" Noah asks as he sits down in front of me at my desk. As much as I know he does not want me to post another video about Tiffany, I have already done it once so might as well to it again. Although the type of response that I received wasn't what I preferred, at least it got her attention. No sense in stopping now.

I begin recording on my phone that is propped up against the lamp on my desk.

"Hi everyone. After hearing about Jesse Jameson's murder in Brookesview and the speculation around Tiffany Burnes being responsible, I wanted to come on here and give my thoughts about everything. I do believe the timing of Jesse's death and location of where he was found is not a coincidence. Although he does not fit her victim profile, I am speculating that something went awry between her and him which ended up leading to his death. Whether Tiffany planned it or not, I do think she is responsible. Again, I do not have confirmation of what happened to Jesse. These are just my thoughts and opinions. Tiffany, when you see this, I want you to know that you will get what's coming for you. Again, my messages are open to anyone who would like to send in anonymous tips regarding Jesse's death or tips relating to the whereabouts of Tiffany Burnes. All tips remain with me and will be withheld from the police unless given permission."

I stop recording and hit post. Either this video will spark a response out of that psycho bitch again, run me out of business, or gain me more clients. And probably a call from Detective Carner too.

2 8

TIFFANY

Bugs are literally crawling over my sneakers and jeans and I can't do anything about it. The storm is getting worse and there is no way that I am going to go hiking out in the rain and lightning.

Funny how the rain can help me in some ways and in other aspects, it becomes a terrible inconvenience. If I was thinking about the rain before coming here, I would have come more equipped and tormenting Ellie would finally come to an end tonight. But that's okay because I like tormenting her, even though I know my fun must come to an end soon.

I had no intention of targeting a man when I was at the bar in Brookesview, but it had been too long since I killed someone before him — a younger man who I attracted a few months before meeting the lawyer who I fought the urge to kill, and that is why killing Jesse was hard to resist, particularly since he was the one who came on to me the other night.

It is Jesse's fault that he died. I was minding my own business, having a drink by myself and contemplating where to spend the night. If he didn't come up to me, he would still be alive.

And that is how I ended up here in the fucking dirt right now. If I resisted the urge to kill that drunk cheater in Brookesview, I would not have to speed up my plans with Ellie. I also would not have to worry about laying low while I stay in Florida.

Once the storm lets up, I will acquire another vehicle again because hiking is getting too exhausting, especially in the fucking rain.

It is as exhausting as it has become to plan out my kills, and I need to save up my energy to finally be done with tormenting Ellie.

2 9

Although I only posted the video last night, there have been no anonymous tips, text messages from Tiffany, or a call from the detective yet.

On my way to Jonesville, a town where Tiffany Burnes grew up which is a three hour long drive from Fairview, I called Ben to see how Cameron was doing. Even though Cameron is supposed to take it easy for the next few weeks, Ben told me they have plans to take him out in a wheelchair to a bar tonight so they can celebrate their friend's birthday. I really don't like the idea of them going out especially after just leaving the hospital so soon, but it's not my place to tell them what to do. I made sure to remind Ben to stay aware of their surroundings and that I am a call or text away if they need me.

Between my own research and what Detective Carner has leniently told me in the beginning of the investigation, I learned Tiffany grew up in Albany, New York with her mother until she died from an overdose when Tiffany was fourteen years old. During the two years following her mother's death, Tiffany was tossed between a few foster homes until a woman named Billie, adopted and raised her from age sixteen into adulthood.

When Billie was questioned by Detective Carner years ago, she claimed she had no idea of her adoptive daughter's killings. Billie said, the last time she had any contact with Tiffany was only a few weeks prior to the night of when everything unfolded.

I take a left off the exit on the highway and continue following my GPS to Billie's house.

I have never spoken to her or her biological daughter, Dianne who is a year older than Tiffany because Detective Carner urged me not to contact either of the two women.

Well until today, I adhered to her request.

In front of me, a one-story blue house sits tucked in between two other houses. I knock on the white painted front door.

A woman who looks to be about in her sixties, dressed in a green robe, blonde hair wrapped around her curlers, slightly opens the door. "Hello. Can I help you?"

"Hello, ma'am. My name is Ellie Moore. I am a local private investigator." I hold out my license toward her. "I am sorry to bother you but I was wondering if I could take a few minutes of your time to ask about—"

"Yes, I know who you are," she answers.

"You do?" I question.

Shit. Did she see the two videos about Tiffany on my social media? I would think she stayed away from the internet after her adoptive daughter turned out to be a killer.

"I saw your website. So, you were the one who figured out who my daughter was?" Billie tilts her head.

Okay, I overlooked my website. My actions always have consequences, I need to remember that.

Now I realize Billie must have looked into investigators to search for Tiffany over these years. Regardless of what kind of psycho Tiffany turned out to be, the woman who raised her would still want to find her. Every family wants an answer, regardless of what it is. With the assumption she had no clue about her adoptive daughter's killings, Billie probably has more questions than all of us do.

"Theoretically," I answer.

"How did you know it was her?"

I clear my throat. "It took the loss of a friend and a lot of risky decisions of mine."

The silence between us is thick for only a brief moment before Billie opens the front door, revealing a full-length green velvet robe that drags to the floor. She gestures toward her home. "Come in."

What a way to get acquainted.

3 0

I never thought about how eerie it would feel to sit in the living room of the house where a serial killer grew up. Then again, I also did not expect for Billie to invite me inside her home either. I wasn't even sure if she was going to answer the front door.

"You said you saw my website. Were you seeking out a P.I. to look for your daughter?"

It is better that I refer to Tiffany as Billie's daughter, rather than saying her name. This shows empathy. Empathizing with Billie will allow her to open up to me and let her guard down a bit. This is a technique that I've learned to make myself seem more compassionate when it comes to getting a witness, or a suspect to give me the answers that I am seeking.

"At first, yes. I searched through the surrounding towns because the few investigators here in Jonesville would not help me. When I read your background under your services, you can understand why I didn't decide to contact you." She hands me a glass of lemonade. "I didn't mean to raise a killer."

"I wasn't thinking that." I sip the lemonade.

"I did my best, really. I had no idea she was capable of such…. atrocities, such… violence," Billie says in broken words, shaking her head.

Murder, you mean?

"I wanted to talk to you about your daughter's childhood. I understand she was in foster care before you adopted her. Did her previous foster parents ever report inappropriate or disruptive behavior out of her as a child?"

Nodding, Billie fixes her robe. "Yes. The first family who fostered her, said she set one of their children's toys on fire in their bathroom. Half the house caught on fire."

"Oh, really?" My interest is peaked. Detective Carner never shared this information with me.

"But that was the only story I've ever heard. She had some trouble with her grades in Senior year. Not a lot of close friends, but she did have *some* friends. Never a best friend though. She wasn't a bad kid. It's not like she was in the principal's office all the time. She isn't a statistic—you know, one of those foster kids who were raised terribly and end up being bad." Tears start flowing down Billie's face as she begins rambling. "I guess I shouldn't say that. H—how could I be so blind? What she did is all my fault. I should have noticed the signs… but as I look back, I can't pick up on anything."

Tiffany growing up to become a murderer is not the direct fault of Billie's, although she feels like it is. Parents are supposed to be responsible for how their children turn out. That's normally how it goes, or is supposed to go. Since I am not a parent and never planned on being one, I don't have any room to talk on the subject. I haven't a clue how I would feel in her situation. I can only imagine and the thought seems unbearable. However, I do relate to Billie when it comes to understanding what it is like to blame yourself for someone's actions, to feel a form of survivor's guilt.

"You started fostering her when she was sixteen, correct?"

Nodding, Billie wipes the tears off her cheeks. "The families who fostered her before me said she was hard to deal with, that she didn't listen. But when I fostered her, I didn't get the same girl they reported. She was pleasant. We had our arguments every now and then but nothing major. When she turned eighteen, she started waitressing to save money to move out. Just before her nineteenth birthday, she wanted her independence and decided to move out on her own. She ended up renting a house out in Avery which I couldn't figure out why she wanted to move there and not stay here in Jonesville..." Billie looks away for a moment before continuing.

"Anyway, the house she ended up renting out was in a nice secluded neighborhood. I thought it was safe for her. I didn't think-- I didn't think she was burying all those men in her yard. I asked her about the artificial grass when I visited once. She said it was to help regrow the grass after the owner had to dig up the yard to fix the sewer system."

What a convenient lie to tell her mother but a thoughtless way to get rid of her victims.

"Did you visit your daughter in Avery often?"

"No. Sadly, she never invited me over after me and my oldest daughter helped her move in." Billie shakes her head. "Now I know why."

"So, she was living in that house for about five years then, huh? The owner must have liked her," I remark.

"I guess so." Billie shrugs. "She never talked about any problems with her landlord. She barely mentioned him to me."

"Him?" I repeat because the name that is listed as the owner or landlord under Tiffany's house in Avery was not a male name. Before Chloe and I broke into Tiffany's house, we googled her address. The name under the property address came back as *Lana Garcia*. I thought Lana was her landlord. "Do you know what her landlords name was?"

"Oh, no I don't. Like I said, she never really mentioned him and I never even got to meet him." Billie shrugs, wiping a tear from her eyes.

"Interesting. Do you know anyone by the name of Lana Garcia?"

Billie shakes her head. "Never heard of that name."

Even more interesting. "Did your daughter have any unusual habits as a teenager? Did she seem likes he had OCD with anything?" A common fact about most killers: they have a form of OCD, something leading to an obsession. Also, they often show no signs of sympathy.

"Oh yes. I used to joke about how clean she kept her room. I'd joke with her that she wasn't a normal messy teenager. She liked the color white. I always thought it was odd because who likes the color white? It gets dirty so quickly."

"I understand." I shift my body, thinking back to Tiffany's white pristine living room.

When Chloe and I broke in, we expected to see proof of a roommate or another family member, rather than realizing Tiffany lived there alone. Billie's colorful messy lived-in living room is the complete opposite of her adoptive daughter's pristine white living room.

The alarm on my phone that is set to remind me it is two o'clock rings. Time to wrap this conversation up already. I show Billie the pink toolbox with the mallet hammer, drill set and other tools that I ordered yesterday, off my phone. "Have you ever seen this toolbox before?"

"No…" Billie squints her eyes as she looks at my screen. "But it reminds me of a toolbox my daughter had in high school. She bought it for a woodworking class in senior year. It was her favorite class. The toolbox came in handy here in the house quite a bit. I'd call her my own handy lady." Billie smiles at the memory as she studies my screen, then reaches out to take my phone. "I remember, one of the hammers in the toolbox transformed into a mini screw driver set. You'd unscrew the handle and inside were five different sized mini screw drivers." She scrolls down a bit, before handing the phone back to me. "This is it. She bought this toolbox in senior year."

On my phone, she shows me a purple toolbox decorated with dark purple hearts that is just slightly bigger than the pink toolbox that I already ordered.

This purple toolbox contains a small purple

hammer with hearts around the handle. It transforms into a set of screw drivers as Billie just described. Besides this tiny transformable hammer, there is an extraction tool set, a purple drill, pink plyers, and the same mallet hammer that comes inside of the pink toolbox.

Billie's face shows that she is now just drawing the same conclusion I was suspecting.

"The detective told me about the weapon and the autopsy on those men," Billie stares past me, shaking her head. "I never thought twice about that toolbox. She took it with her when she moved out and I never saw it again… I didn't associate the tools with what she did." Billie begins crying, frantically shaking as she stammers. "Why… why didn't I make that connection? I need to call the Detective and tell her…"

When you are not around a person twenty-four seven, there can be a lot you don't know about them, regardless of who they are and how close of a relationship you two share. I definitely learned this when I thought I knew who Chloe was before truly getting to actually know her.

I can tell that Billie didn't know what heinous crimes Tiffany was committing. The pain and confusion shows in her eyes. Her emotions are raw and not rehearsed. But what about her biological daughter, Dianne? How close was she to Tiffany? Did she know what she was doing?

"I'm sorry to cause you such pain with this conversation," I say. "I'll be going soon but may I ask you, where is your oldest daughter, Dianne at right now? Does she still live with you?"

By the looks of the house, it seems as if another

person lives here and I am guessing it's Dianne.

"Yes. She's a flight attendant so she's barely home but she stays with me when she's in town. She's working right now. You can give her a call later on, if you want to speak with her. I'll give you her phone number."

I decline to accept her number because Billie gave me more information during this visit than I expected she would. Also, if I am going to question Dianne, it needs to be in person than on the phone. "One last question, do you have a recent photo of Tiffany?"

"No, sadly I don't. She never liked photos of herself. The most recent one I took of her was on her eighteen birthday." Billie wipes away her tears, sniffling. "She wouldn't even let me take a picture with her before she moved out."

That explains why the detective used the photo I secretly took of Tiffany in the bar to show the public. It also shows that Tiffany knew what she was doing. No photos can lead to no proof of her existence. I thank Billie for her time and apologize for any hurt I have caused during our difficult conversation.

When I leave her house, I merge onto the highway toward the exit for Avery. Since I will be passing the town on my way back to Fairview, I want to stop and pay a visit to Tiffany's old house one last time.

3 1

January 13th
10:30 a.m.

The crime scene tape that once surrounded the perimeter of Tiffany's front yard has been removed. I expected the owner to have rented this house out by now or at least put it up on the market for sale after what happened with Tiffany, except there isn't a for rent or for sale sign anywhere.

My intention in coming here was to only drive by. I did not plan to get out of my truck until my feet took the lead toward the front door, an all too reminiscent memory of my same actions years ago. Except back then, Chloe was lingering behind me.

I peer through the window next to the front door and see the curtains are pulled back. What I last saw of a perfectly pristine white living room has turned into an empty unkept abandoned house. Dirty footprints from the shoes of the crime scene team and law enforcement cover the once clean white rug.

I know this is not a good idea, but again, my feet take over before my mind can. I walk away from the front door to go to the backyard where Chloe and I broke in through the back gate. The lock Chloe lockpicked is no longer here, allowing me to walk right into the backyard. The artificial grass which encased Tiffany's victims is gone and is now replaced with mounds of dirt. The green furniture on her porch is torn up and dirty from all the recent rain.

I wonder, what do the neighbors think? When Chloe and I broke into the back of this yard back then, nobody saw us because the nearest neighbors are not that close by. There are two mobile homes on each side of this house and they are about five-hundred feet apart from each other. Both houses have fenced-in backyards like this one, so nobody was able to see us when we were breaking in. Nobody ever came out of either house during the time we waited for paramedics and police to arrive either.

I would imagine, if Detective Carner did her job properly, that she spoke to them. If someone happened to see or know something about Tiffany, the neighbors would be the most helpful. After all, your neighbors usually know more about you than you think they do. I knew about all of my neighbors back in Avery when they didn't even know me. Look where that got me today.

Detective Carner never told me whether she questioned the neighbors about Tiffany afterwards because I never asked her. I just assumed she spoke to them because why wouldn't she?

I leave the house to get back in my truck. Then I drive down the road to park in the driveway of one of the neighbors. There is a car in the driveway, so I am hoping that somebody is home.

After knocking on the red door and waiting a minute, I introduce myself to a woman who looks roughly thirty years older than me. Her cell phone is pressed to her right ear, held up by her right shoulder.

"Sorry to bother you. If I could take a moment of your time to ask a few questions about your previous neighbor, Tiffany—"

"Oh, that psycho who used to live next to me?" Scrunching her forehead, the woman holds up her pointer finger, signalling for me to wait as she speaks into the phone. "I'll call you back." She steps out onto the porch and closes the door behind her and sits in one of the two red chairs out here. "You aren't the first person whose stopped by here, ma'am."

"Today?" I sit down in the other available seat.

"No, not today. I mean, in general, over these years. A slew of reporters came knocking on my door ever since that woman made the news. Nobody has come by in a couple months until you just did though. I don't think a private investigator has ever knocked on my door, now that I think about it. You're the first one. Just nosey reporters."

The thought of a bunch of reporters showing up to her doorstep is unfathomable since this town is so small. Then again, Tiffany Burnes is wanted nationwide. Every reporter wants to cover her story. No matter how far they have to travel to get it.

"So, what do you want to know about her? Truthfully, I don't know much but I can attempt to help you out and answer your questions."

"I appreciate your willingness to help. How long

have you been living here?"

"Fifteen years."

"Wow, that's a long time. You live alone?"

"I inherited this place when my dad died. Raised my two daughters here. A year ago, my husband and I retired."

"That must be nice. Were you both home the morning of when the crime investigation team came to Tiffany's house?"

"No, my husband and I were on vacation that week. I'm sad to say we missed out on all the action. Never had anything interesting happen here in this sleepy little neighborhood until that day. I didn't even know anything was going on until my friend called me and said my street was on the news. It is crazy to think, I lived next to a serial killer and I hadn't a clue about what she was doing. Scary to think about!"

"Oh yeah, I'm sure that day was something to gossip about." I smile. "Since you've been living here awhile, you lived here when Tiffany first rented her house out then. Do you remember seeing her move in?"

"Yes. I remember it was about five years ago when I first saw her. She was very young. I figured she was Frederick's granddaughter – the man who lived in the house before her, because I never saw a *for rent* sign up in his yard before she moved in. I figured Frederick passed away and she took over the house because one day, Frederick was there and then I started seeing Tiffany. Soon, I just stopped seeing Frederick. I wanted to ask her about him, but never got the chance. If I tried to get her attention, she'd always act like she didn't see me. I just figured she wasn't friendly."

"Did you ever see her and Frederick together or only separately?"

"I saw them together only once. They were getting out of his car one morning."

"Interesting. Did you know Frederick well? Can you tell me a little bit about him?"

"Oh, no I didn't know him too well. He was an elderly man, about in his eighties. He had been living in this neighborhood for at least a decade before me and my husband moved here. Could have even been living here longer than that. He always kept to himself. Nice old man from the few times we spoke."

If he lived here for over a decade, then why isn't his name listed as the property owner or landlord?

"Have you heard of the name Lana Garcia?" I ask her.

Nodding, she answers. "That was Frederick's wife. He told me she passed away a few years before I moved here."

Okay, so that explains the name of the property owner online then. After Lana died, Frederick probably never switched the homeowner's name to his. It would make sense that after living in the house for so many years, that it would have been paid off by then. So there was more than likely, no need to switch homeowner names.

"Did you ever notice if Tiffany had any roommates or a boyfriend living with her at any time?"

"I don't recall ever seeing another person live there except her. Nothing ever seemed out of the ordinary to me. She was a very quiet neighbor, but not friendly at all." Shaking her head, the woman rolls her eyes. "Now I understand why. I used to get irritated when she gave me the cold shoulder whenever we'd drive by each other. I'd try to wave but like I said, she would normally act like she didn't see me."

Of course, she would. I thank the woman whose name I rudely failed to get, before walking back to my truck. I decide against knocking on the house to the left of Tiffany's because the hurricane shutters were down and there weren't any vehicles parked in the driveway: Two clear signs no one was home.

While driving on the highway to get back to Fairview, I focus at my rearview mirrors more often than at the road in front of me. A grey car has been driving behind me in the same lane on the highway for a mile and a half now. Time to switch to the middle lane and see if they follow.

I breathe a sigh of relief when the driver speeds by me. Ten miles down, a black SUV follows closely behind, practically driving right on my bumper. I switch back over to the right lane and the vehicle swerves around me.

At the Fairview exit, I veer onto the off-ramp to get off the highway. Three miles down, I make a right off of the populated road and onto a one-lane road that needs an updated pavement job. Five minutes later, I approach the entrance to the dirt road where my mailbox is and double check there are no vehicles trailing far behind me. Then I turn my own headlights off before making the turn. A hundred feet down, I turn my headlights back on.

If the psycho bitch followed me to Avery once, I should expect that she's been following me everywhere.

And I am hoping she did all the way to Jonesville today. From my conversation with Billie, it is clear they didn't have much trouble in their mother daughter relationship which means Tiffany could have a soft spot for her adoptive mother.

Serial killers normally show a lack of human connectiveness, a lack of understanding compassion for their victims. But just because they show lack of empathy and sympathy, killers can still have weaknesses too. Maybe Billie is hers, and inadvertently, I think I might be using that to my advantage.

It's dangerous when you start thinking like a killer.

3 2

January 13th
1:00 p.m.

In my office, I search online for a deceased record on *Frederick Garcia*. Instead, a list of men in various age ranges who are still alive come up in the results. One of the profiles match the age range he would be today which would be *ninety-five*, and it states Frederick is still alive.

A background check reveals early criminal reports of drunken behavior when he was in his thirties, but no other criminal or arrest records have been reported since then. He held an occupation as a dentist for forty years before retiring seventeen years ago. He is widowed by Lana Garcia who passed away twenty years ago. Besides Lana, I cannot find any information about Frederick's distant or immediate family online. As the neighbor said, Frederick kept to himself and from my online findings, she was telling me the truth.

It also says he currently resides at the address in Avery but that hasn't been true since

Tiffany moved in years ago. So then if he is still alive and has no family left, a widowed elderly man in his nineties could only be in a handful of places: a hospital, an assisted living facility, a nursing home, or a retirement centre.

I strike out on my luck when calling both hospitals, so I move on to call the only retirement home, and two assisted living facilities in Avery.

By the fifth call, I am back to square one. There is no record of Frederick Garcia in any of them. The search for *'nursing homes'* only yields me the same results that come up for the retirement centre. Although he isn't in Avery, Frederick could be in one of those facilities or a hospital in another town or state.

That is, if he is still alive. There are no deceased records online, but it doesn't mean that he's still alive. If he was killed and nobody was around to report his death or see him die, nobody would know. With no family or friends to report him missing or if there is no evidence of him dying, then Frederick Garcia remains alive to the public. There would be no death record to prove he's gone.

On my board, I place a post-it note that says **Frederick Garcia** written in Sharpie and a question mark. Then another note beneath it: *Widowed elderly man / no family. Vanished five years ago when Tiffany moved in. What was his connection to Tiffany?*

Tiffany's plans to murder did not just come to her overnight. It's obvious she meticulously planned out how she would get away with all her crimes by the burial in her yard that was once Frederick's yard. Tiffany had the confidence of thinking nobody would ever catch onto her which is why I believe she chose Frederick's backyard for a burial ground. It was the perfect area, a house out in the woods with barely any neighbors around, and he was the perfect target, an unsuspecting elderly man who she could easily seduce or maybe only persuade.

Frederick sounds like he was the perfect target for a young Tiffany Burnes, particularly if she hadn't had any or little experience in murder yet. If I were as deranged as Tiffany and had the same motive, I would have killed him and taken over his house.

The neighbor who spoke to me never saw a for rent sign because Frederick's house was never up for rent in the first place.

But he wasn't found amongst the eight male victims found in her backyard years ago, so then what did Tiffany do with him?

Better question, what would I do with him?

3 3

Waking up to a call from Ben Robinson at three o'clock this morning was not how I imagined the start of my day would go. Especially after only falling asleep about two hours before the phone rang.

"I'm sorry to wake you up at this time, but me and Cameron just got home and our place is trashed. Someone broke-in while we were gone, but it's a little strange because nothing is stolen. Everything's accounted for. Computer and Xbox are still here. TV's here too, even though it's face down on the fucking floor. I don't get it. Nobody would target us like this, so I don't know who could have done this. You told me to call you if anything strange happened and well, uh, I guess you could say, this is pretty strange," Ben told me over the phone. He assured me that he and Cameron were safe in their apartment and he didn't sound too worried, but rather skeptical of the situation. I knew they shouldn't have gone out for their friend's birthday tonight especially after Cameron just got released from the hospital only two days ago. Then again if they did stay home, what would have happened to them instead?

I told Ben to call the police because even though nothing seems to be stolen, whoever trashed their place, somehow broke in and still committed a crime. However, Ben had no intentions of wanting to deal with the police again and I did not disagree with him. So, I insisted on paying for a hotel for the next two nights to ensure their safety and they agreed.

I just pulled into the parking lot of their apartment complex. With no enemies and the photo Tiffany sent me of them, I don't think that their break-in was a coincidence. But there is also not much more for me to do besides check them into a hotel with good security cameras and a security guard on the premises. In their apartment, I show them the photo Tiffany took in the hospital. Then we'll see if they change their minds about calling the police. Telling Ben over the phone would do him no good other than worry, so might as well tell him in person. I hope my lack of information will not deter their trust in me after this.

Noah, who did not take no for an answer once he volunteered himself to come with me, promised to remain in my truck while I go inside their apartment.

I walk to the fifth door on the first floor of their two-story apartment complex and take note of no surveillance system on the building. If it were not in the middle of the night, a neighbor could have possibly seen or heard the break-in, had it happened a few hours earlier. Then it would be appropriate for me to knock on their doors and ask around. However, not at nearly four o'clock in the morning, it's not.

Ben opens the door and invites me inside of their apartment. My eyes immediately lock onto the broken glass from the TV on the floor. The cushions are ripped out of the sofa and on the ground next to the TV. Food and plates scatter the kitchen counter and tile floor where Cameron sits, quietly scrolling on his phone in a wheelchair at the dining room table.

"I wasn't being honest with you when we spoke on the phone while you were in the hospital the other day," I say to Cameron and get ready to show them their photo on my phone. "I called to ask you how you were doing but I was also calling to make sure you two were safe. Tiffany Burnes sent me this photo of you two while you were still being treated in the hospital." Ben stops cleaning up and walks over to me and Cameron. They both look at my phone in shock.

"What the fuck?" Ben gasps, forehead scrunched. "What the fuck?" he repeats.

"I waited to tell you guys about this because I didn't want you to be worried while you were still in the hospital. Since you told me you had plans to go out tonight, I didn't want to frighten you with this photo." I clear my throat, knowing how incredibly thoughtless my words are sounding. *Don't be worried that a serial killer who specifically targets men was outside your door, taking a photo of you while you were both asleep.*

"You couldn't have at least asked a security guard or someone to watch our door that night?" Ben asks.

"Theoretically yes, but it wouldn't have been as simple as you think," I answer and turn my attention to Cameron. "That's why I called you as soon as I received the photo. I'm sorry if I mishandled this situation but honestly, I did not feel like you two were in danger that night. Once I received the message, I called you right away and confirmed she was not in the area. I believe she sent the photo to simply warn me that she is back. If Tiffany had any intentions to harm you two, she would have done so or attempted to do so that night in the hospital. But we can still go to the police station together to report it, if you don't want to go to the hotel anymore." I direct my attention to Ben. "My strategy may seem a little unethical, but please trust that I have your safety and best interest in mind."

"Nah. Fuck the police. We'll go to the hotel tonight." Cameron's response tells me that he is not pleased about the police's response to when he went missing. To think, if Ben never contacted me, Cameron would most likely would have died in those woods by now. "We trust you, Ellie." Cameron nods.

"I really appreciate that." I begin looking around their apartment as Ben gets things ready for the hotel. There is no note or hint of a clue that was left from Tiffany. No type of cryptic message laying around waiting for me to find. Then again, there wouldn't be a clue or message for me here. I should be expecting a text message if she were responsible for this after all and I have not received one yet. The more I inspect the place, I remain confused about why Tiffany would choose to trash it.

She's not a serial trasher. She's a serial killer. Breaking and throwing things around is not Tiffany's scene.

Is she the person that is even responsible for this

after all?

Given Cameron's history with drug abuse, my mind goes to the obvious. He could have enemies from during the time of his addiction in the past. Maybe someone came in here to ransack his apartment for drugs or money.

But no, I should not start doubting my client now especially since he has not given me anything to doubt him on before. And if life has taught me anything, coincidences are not always so coincidental.

If Tiffany broke-into their apartment with the intention to kill them, that means her plan went awry which most likely provoked her to dismantle everything in their apartment. Cameron only left the hospital yesterday. I presume Tiffany thought he would be home tonight. She arrived to kill both of them, if not only one, then resulted to a fit of rage when realizing they weren't home...

Think like a killer...

If I were Tiffany and my plan failed tonight, I still wouldn't have revealed that I broke-in by breaking and throwing things around, especially since the plan failed. I would want to come back again, so giving myself away is not a smart move... but creating a distraction from who I really want to target is.

Somehow Tiffany knew I would come running over to protect my clients which means this was a set up to get me away from something. The only two things that Tiffany would want to distract me from would be my husband and my own home.

<h1 style="text-align:center">3 4</h1>

<h1 style="text-align:center">T I F F A N Y</h1>

Seeing Ellie squirm was fascinating as she rushed to save her clients like the vigilante that she thinks she is. I did not expect to see Noah tagging along with her. However, his choice of being overprotective ended up working out even better in my favor.

Moments like tonight, remind me of the first time I killed a man. Particularly, since he has been haunting my dreams lately. That night I killed him didn't end how I thought it would, but it turned out even better! The first time I felt true happiness was that night and because of Ellie, that happiness *almost* got taken away from me forever.

After I took that idiots life with his own lamp, I realized that I needed to be well equipped for the next time I'd kill a man. There was no sense in running the risk of getting caught even though I already got away with it once, so I needed to be prepared.

Relying on whatever object nearby at the time

for a weapon would put me at risk. What if there were no lamps beside the next guy? I needed to always have something on me that would be strong enough to defend myself. A gun was out of the question because those are loud and not as fun. I liked having direct contact with my victim. A gun would make killing too easy, too fast.

I needed something unique, cute, heavy, reliable, and the perfect size— like me. And most importantly, it needed to be small enough to carry in my purse.

I had just graduated high school three months before I succeeded at killing my first victim. I had already been looking for an apartment to move out on my own. Not that I didn't enjoy living with Billie. Out of all foster parents, she was the best one. But I needed my own freedom as every young adult does. When I was cleaning out my room one day, still pondering the thought of how to proceed with my newfound therapy, I realized I already had the perfect weapon to get me started.

The thought of using it for murder never crossed my mind until then.

Once checking off the proper weapon, the next thing on my list was to find a burial place for my victims. Leaving them at the scene of the crime permits greater risk at implicating me in their murder. That's why most killers often get caught. They don't have a sacred place to bury their trophies.

My bedroom was my sacred place at the time, but I knew Billie's house could not be an option. My own house would be though. What better place to bury a body than the backyard of my own home, right? Such as a place where no one would ever be invited over or would ever expect to look. That's when I shifted my search from looking at apartments to house hunting, before realizing that renting a house was out of my eighteen-year-old budget.

Using my beauty to my advantage hadn't been a stranger to me before. So when my elderly customer, Frederick, began showing up every morning during my work shift at the diner, who often spoke about his lovely home in the next town over, he became my perfect target. For a $3.50 cup of coffee a morning, he'd drop me a ten-dollar tip. That would happen every morning at 6:00 a.m. for eight months just before I got off my overnight shift. And before leaving the diner just as I was getting ready to get off work myself, he would always tell me to 'have a good day, beautiful.' To which I would wink and tell him, 'you always make my day!'

Through various coffee visits at the diner, he told me his life story. Frederick was a widowed old man who lived in Avery which was only a fifteen-minute drive from Jonesville where the diner that I worked at was located. He lived in the woods and only had two neighbors beside him. He also told me his wife died of some disease I never cared to hear about.

Frederick enjoyed talking to me and trusted me so much that he offered for me to stay in his house when I "couldn't find a place to crash after fighting with my mom," before getting off my work shift one morning. Since I already knew his wife passed away and he had no one to talk to, I knew he couldn't turn me down and of course, he wouldn't want to. No man ever wants to turn me down. That's why killing them is so easy.

I did not enjoy using Billie in my lie and I never

did it again after that one time. Billie always treated me right and I miss her a lot. I even miss Dianne who I tried hating at first. But Dianne just ended up being that kind of person who forcefully makes you like her in a good way. She never gave in to my stupid antics as a teenager. She brushed me off and told me I'd eventually love her and the loving bitch ended up being right.

The mere thought of never being able to contact Billie and Dianne ever again, fuels my rage toward Ellie even more. The closest people to me have been taken away because of her. I would love to take Ellie away from her own family too, but she is too cold to care about her estranged parents.

Who Ellie cares about most is her husband and random men that she's never met before; my prime and easy targets.

3 5

January 14th
5:00 a.m.

Ben and Cameron followed me in their own car to a hotel on the other side of town. I made sure to keep my eyes on the rearview mirrors in case Tiffany decided to follow them in another stolen vehicle. With all the right turns I took on the secluded roads we drove on, spotting the same vehicle behind us would have been easy to notice.

While I was checking Cameron and Ben into the hotel, Noah sped through all of the recordings from our security cameras during the last few hours on his phone. I told him about my assumption of Tiffany creating some sort of distraction to get me away from him or the house, possibly even both. That is, if she didn't react out of rage upon learning Ben and Cameron weren't home.

Although, I am rethinking my assumptions because the last recording shows us rushing out of the front door to leave for my client's apartment.

The tires on my truck kick the dirt up from the road as I am pulling into my driveway. The headlights of my truck illuminate our front yard, an eerie and appropriate silence fills the air as Noah and I get out to head toward our front door.

Even though the last recording is of us and I trust my security system, something tells me to draw my gun before Noah unlocks and opens the door. I am confident in my property's security system which has not alerted me of any suspicious activity during the time we were gone, but we can't put anything by Tiffany. Noah inserts the key, turns the doorknob, and opens the door. I step in front of him to walk inside of the house first.

He lingers behind me, focusing his attention on his phone. Each room that has a camera inside of the house is displayed in a grid on his screen: our living room, kitchen, backyard, and the hallway which shows the doors to our offices, bathroom, and bedroom. Tiffany is not anywhere on these cameras.

Cautiously, I walk through the entryway. I make my way through the living room, through the kitchen and into the hallway to check the four rooms without surveillance: our bedroom, bathroom, my office, and Noah's office.

Before opening the bedroom door, I remember Noah's gun is in the nightstand on his side of the bed. If Tiffany somehow got in there undetected, which should be impossible, she could have access to his weapon and I might be facing a real gun fight. There is a strong possibility that I might not be the only one who is armed in my own house.

"Open the door," I whisper to Noah and after he does, I step into the bedroom and flip on the light switch off the wall.

Nobody, let alone Tiffany is in here. The window is still shut and locked, just like we left it.

I walk back out of the bedroom and across the hall to check Noah's office before going into mine which is right next to his, then into the bathroom at the end of the hall.

No sign of Tiffany and each room seems to be left untouched. After concluding there isn't a threat or a disturbance in my home, I go into the living room and place my weapon safely in my purse. I slump down on the couch. "I don't get it. What else would make Tiffany decide to trash Ben and Cameron's apartment, if it wasn't to distract me?"

"How could she have known that they would call you and not the police anyways?" Noah makes a good point, but as I have to remember, we can't put anything past Tiffany. Whether the situation makes sense or not.

"I don't know, but who else would trash their apartment and not steal anything? I believe Ben when he said nobody would target them. I don't know. Nothing is making sense..." I look around the living room. There is no sign of Tiffany anywhere in here and besides what my own eyes are telling me, my cameras already proved that before we walked in the front door. So why do I feel like someone is here right now? Or at least, recently was?

"Maybe the bitch got angry because Ben and Cameron weren't home, like you said in the car," Noah says as he sits next to me.

"I was just speculating on the way here, but if you think about it, that theory doesn't make sense either. If that were the case, then why didn't she just wait for them to come back home if she had plans to kill them to begin with?" I place myself inside of Tiffany's mind. It's possible their absence sent her into a fury, but again, causing a mess is not her scene.

"She hid in Chloe's bathroom and murdered her with no problem. The investigative team said she must have been hiding out in the shower that night before killing Chloe because of the position they found her body in. If Tiffany was that confident to wait for Chloe in her own home and kill her that way, then I don't see what would have stopped her from killing Ben and Cameron in the same way she killed Chloe."

"Because this time, there were two of them and not one?" Noah suggests as more of a question than a tailored thought.

"That's not a viable theory either because if she arrived to their apartment with the intention of both Cameron and Ben being home in the first place, then that doesn't make any sense. If Tiffany's sole intent was to kill both of them, or even just one of them, there was nothing stopping her tonight. Just like there was nothing stopping her from getting to them at the hospital. This was her second chance to harm them and she didn't."

I open Tiffany's most recent messages on my phone and realize she said one other important thing that I have not been focusing on. Because of Ben and Cameron's photo, I looked over what she said about my video.

Your video won't help you at all.

"My video showed her that I'm not taking her threats as seriously as she wants me to. That's why she texted me their photo. She wants me to know how untouchable she still is by threatening the people around me," I say to Noah who is looking helplessly confused as I ramble. "There is nobody in my life that is worth threatening who is especially a male besides you, Ben and Cameron. In Tiffany's mindset, sending me a photo of my clients in the hospital would hit a nerve with me, but once she saw that I posted a second video not backing down from her, she realized it didn't."

Noah is clearly not following anything I just said, yet at the same time trying to be supportive. "You sure you don't want to call Detective Carner yet?"

"Not yet. Ben and Cameron are safe in the hotel for tonight and tomorrow. I alerted the hotel security to keep an eye on their room and they all know to call me if they see her. Ben is also legally armed. They're both on extra alert since I was honest with them about the photo. They can handle themselves."

"Ellie, one of them has broken legs." Noah sighs.

"I know that, but I'm not going to let anybody close to me get hurt by that bitch again. Just trust me."

3 6

Assuming Jesse fell victim to Tiffany, the opportunity to kill must have presented itself upon meeting him. If that's the case, I believe she was in Brookesview to lay low while she is busy stalking me. Avery, Fairview, and Brookesview are all neighboring towns with Fairview being in the middle. Even though Tiffany disguises herself very well, she still runs too high of a risk in getting noticed if she stays in one place too long.

Although it hasn't been confirmed whether Tiffany is behind Jesse Jameson's murder or not, I can only assume that if she was responsible, something awry happened between them.

Tiffany cannot plan out her murders like she was used to doing in Avery. She doesn't have an attic to drug, bludgeon, and chop up her victims, along with a burial ground in her backyard anymore. Because of me, she hasn't had any of that for years now. I believe she didn't plan to kill anyone while she came back to

Florida — not when she's busy tormenting me. Then I can also assume, whatever plans she has with me, will be fulfilled soon.

From what Detective Carner said to me over the phone, Jesse lied about his outing with coworkers the night he was murdered. It seems like the man was out to cheat and his infidelity led him to Tiffany. I'm not saying death should be the consequence of cheating, but karma is a bitch.

Then again, I won't know anything for certain until Detective Carner gives me a call or makes a statement to the public. Whatever comes first. That is, if either ever does. But I do know, Tiffany must have her murder weapon still.

On my board, photos of the purple toolbox with the mallet hammer are tacked next to the note — MURDER WEAPON?

The package with the pink toolbox and the steel hole puncher that I ordered the other day, arrived a few minutes ago. I wish I talked to Billie before placing the order because then I would have ordered the purple toolbox that Tiffany bought instead. But at least I still have what is most important; the same mallet hammer Tiffany has, which comes in both toolboxes.

Billie confirmed Tiffany's purchase of the hammer and not the hole puncher, but since I already bought the puncher before talking to Billie, I might as well see what the hole puncher can do too.

In my front yard, I slam the puncher against the tree trunk in front of me. It doesn't leave a mark, so I try again with more force. Nothing.

I pull the mallet hammer out of the box and

handle it the same way when swinging it against the tree. This time, it leaves an imprint of a heart into the bark. My tape measure tells me it's exactly two inches wide, confirming the measurements are true to the details listed on the shop's website.

"Ellie! You out here?" My name is being called from the front of the house. Noah probably wants me to come inside for dinner. I bet he's also wondering what the hell I'm doing out here too.

As I leave the side of my house and walk back around to the front yard, I examine the hammer in my hand. Since Tiffany bought this same one when she was a teenager, I wonder if she already had an idea to kill with it to begin with.

Investigators said one of the bodies that were found in her backyard was killed about five years ago and likely her first victim. That would have made her nineteen years old; a year after she graduated high school. That was also the same year she moved into Frederick's house. Except her earliest victim wasn't identified as Frederick because of his age None of those victims in the yard were over the age of thirty at their time of death.

But Frederick's sudden absence from his house and Tiffany's appearance, just doesn't add up.

Think like a killer.

My thought process brings me to when I found Cameron. My gut instinct told me that if anything out of the ordinary were to happen to him on his route home, it would be in the woods, and I was right.

I thought the same way when I was secretly investigating Chloe before we became friends. I assumed she was burying her bodies in the woods because her house lined up to the woods, just like Tiffany's backyard did.

The woods are a perfect place to bury a body if you know what you're doing… or even if you don't.

3 7

January 15th
2:02 a.m.

An alarm echoes throughout the house, waking me and Noah up from an abrupt sleep. I reach over to grab my gun out of my nightstand drawer, and Noah reaches for his over on his side. He is quicker to retrieve his gun, and get out of bed before me because he sleeps closer to the door.

"Wait!" I stop him while quickly picking my phone up off the nightstand to look at my security camera app.

But as I'm pulling up the app, the alarm suddenly stops blaring. The front and back doors are both shut and no one is in the living room, kitchen, and hallway as I view the cameras on my phone. I swipe over to enlarge the view of the front yard and backyard.

"Nobody's in the house. I don't see anyone outside either." I tell Noah who opens the bedroom door to walk out into the hallway.

I follow him out of the bedroom and go to check the bathroom at the end of the hall while he checks my office.

We meet back in the hallway, shaking our heads. The last room to check is his office which is directly across from our bedroom.

Nobody's here. "I don't get it. Why would the alarm suddenly stop without us stopping it?" I think aloud to Noah as I walk over toward the window in his office. We have tiny motion sensors on every window in the house, so when you slide it open, an alarm goes off. I'm not sure if we were awoken by one of the sensors or the actual alarm system on the house because we haven't heard either since we moved in and tested everything. The window is closed and locked shut while the sensor is still switched to the on position. If it were off, then I'd know an intruder came in.

I move on to check every other room in the house, starting with the double pane living room window, the kitchen window, the sliding backdoor, and my office window. They all remain shut, locked, and each motion sensor is still set to on. Our bathroom window doesn't even open because for some reason, the owner before us glued it shut. We haven't shelled out the money to fix it yet.

"Maybe the security alarm just got tripped on its own. The system hasn't been installed that long. It could be faulty. Something probably set it off," Noah says.

"The security system has been installed for two years now and that's never happened once." I mutter, placing my gun on the living room table with the muzzle pointed toward the wall, then slumping down on the couch behind it.

Installing the security cameras was the first thing

Noah did the day we moved in. When we were starting to get settled in about a month after, he installed an alarm system on the front and back doors, and we added separate motion sensors on every window. The security alarm only rings whenever a camera stops working, or if a door opens while the alarm system on the house is set. We also receive an alert on our phones through an app.

If a window opens while the sensors are switched to the on position, the alarm on that window will go off. My security app on my phone didn't alert me or Noah's phone but the motion sensors are all switched to *on,* so we must've heard the house system… but why didn't it alert us on our phones too?

"What would set the alarm off without anyone blatantly breaking in through the front or back door?" I think aloud as Noah looks around the living room, puzzled. None of the furniture is disturbed and nothing was stolen. Then again, if Tiffany were here, what would she want to take?

She wouldn't steal anything, just like she didn't steal anything in Cameron and Ben's apartment. Her interest is not to steal anything. The only difference with their break-in and mine: she trashed their place and mine remains untouched.

"Come with me to my office so we can look through the cameras on a bigger screen," I suggest to my husband. "If someone tried to break-in from outside and that's what woke us up, then the cameras had to have caught them. We just need to skim through the footage and see what we find."

In my office, I scrub through sped up footage of the past few hours through all five of our outdoor cameras. It isn't until I rewind the footage back to the time of seven o'clock last night, when I see myself walk out of the front door with the pink toolbox.

I click over to enlarge the camera that views the side of our house where mine and Noah's office windows are. I watch myself walk into the camera frame for a moment before heading toward the woods on the side of the house. The tree that I chose to utilize with my new toolbox, must be in a blind spot of that camera out there because I don't see myself performing the actions with the hammer and hole puncher on the screen.

Ten minutes later, we see Noah open the front door. He calls my name to come inside for dinner. Four minutes after that, I walk back into the camera frame on the side of the house with only the hammer in my hand. That hammer should still be sitting in my desk drawer…

And as I open the drawer right now in my office, I confirm it remains exactly where I put it.
I left the rest of the tools in the toolbox with the steel hole puncher by the tree because I planned to go back outside after dinner to keep experimenting. But then it started raining, so I ended up leaving everything out there. It's not like anyone is around to steal anything. At least that was my belief until now.

"Where are you going?" Noah watches me get up from my desk, then follows me out of my office.

"I need to check something." I grab my gun off the living room table before walking toward the front door to put my shoes on.

"Ellie!" Noah calls after me, but I am already opening the front door with my flashlight shining from my phone in one hand, and my gun in the other.

Noah, who is armless because he left his gun in the kitchen and probably for the better, quickly follows me outside as I round the corner toward the woods on the side of the house. "Where are you going? Come back inside! It's about to start pouring out here!"

Ignoring him and the budding thunder, I continue walking toward the tree where the toolbox and its contents should still be.

Shining my flashlight in its direction, I approach the area on the side of the house where I was last night, except I don't see a thing. I am certain this was the last place I left everything though. Not only by memory, but also because the camera footage from last night proved it when I walked back in the house with only the hammer.

"Did you pick up a toolbox that was out here?" I turn around to ask Noah.

He shakes his head, forehead scrunched. "What toolbox are you talking about?"

3 8

T I F F A N Y

"Wait, what about a toolbox?" I hear Noah ask Ellie. "Ellie, what are you doing? What are you talking about?"

"I left a toolbox outside in the front yard on the tree we were just at. It's not there anymore."

Ellie's office door just opened; their voices becoming more distinct.

"One of my toolboxes?" He questions her.

"No!" The frustration rises in her voice. "I bought my own toolbox the other day. It has Tiffany's murder weapon in it."

"What the fuck?" Noah gasps. "What do you mean?"

"It's not the same one as hers, but it's what she uses. You know how I told you about the heart shaped weapon she used to bludgeon her victims? I found out that she bought a toolbox in high school and it had a mallet hammer with a heart engraved on the face of it. I bought a similar toolbox with the same hammer from the same shop. Look."

Thump. Slide.

"This is the hammer that I think she uses to kill her victims. I left the rest of the tools and the toolbox outside by the tree last night, but none of it's there anymore."

"How did you figure out that this is what she uses?"

"I did a lot of research."

There she goes, deceiving her husband again. If he only knew she were driving around in my hometown, and had the nerve to step foot in my old house when she knew I was watching her.

"And you think she was outside and stole the toolbox?"

"Who else would have taken it?"

"I don't know but if she already has her own hammer, then why would she want to take your toolbox if the hammer wasn't even in it? What else was in that?"

A steel hole puncher that I never knew I needed until Ellie just supplied it to me.

"There were some other tools, but it doesn't matter what else was left out there. She probably didn't realize the hammer wasn't inside of it. I bet she just grabbed the toolbox and didn't take the time to look through it."

"And you're sure you left the toolbox outside near that tree last night?"

"Yes, Noah! You just saw me on the cameras yourself. I walked out of the house with it and then I came back in for dinner when you called me. I had the hammer in my hand. I put it in my drawer before we sat down to eat. The hammer's still here."

"Why didn't you tell me that was what you were doing? You said you went outside to the clean the windows."

"I'm sorry, but did you really think I was outside cleaning?"

Noah huffs. "Were you going to tell me about the toolbox if it didn't go missing tonight?"

"Yes, but I wasn't done experimenting."

"Okay, well then we need to make a police report," he says.

"And tell them what? That our security alarm went off in the middle of the night, and even though there is no evidence of an intruder besides a missing tool box, we think a serial killer was here?"

"Then what do you want to do, Ellie?"

"I need to keep looking through the camera footage again, then I'll decide."

Good luck wasting your time.

"Okay, let me start making us some coffee."

"No, you need to get back to sleep. You have a meeting in a few hours." Ellie's voice echoes from the office. "I'll be fine in here."

"Alright, but come wake me up if you hear anything."

Like Ellie will be able to wake Noah up. He sleeps through everything except an alarm which I am so mad at myself for setting off. Ellie is the one who wanders around restless and hinders my activities which is fitting because she's Ellie. Of course, she is going to interrupt my plans without even knowing she is interrupting them.

If I never accidentally set the alarm off tonight, things would look a lot differently for her and Noah right now. If only they knew they can thank me for another day of living.

The shine from this brand new single steel hole puncher glistens in my hands. I've never seen it before but thanks to Ellie, I am glad it's mine now. This thing is just as useful as my hammer is. Which speaking of, seeing Ellie's new pink toolbox was a bit shocking. How did she know I have the same one? I'm not a pink girl though. I didn't expect Ellie to be either. What did she think she was going to do with this anyways?

Doesn't matter to me because now I can thank her for my new gift. Instead of one weapon, I now have two. See what I mean about our love hate relationship?

3 9

January 15th
8:00 a.m.

There are two types of serial killers: Those who go on killing sprees based off an emotion. Then there are those who like to plan their crimes out carefully. However often times, the killers who prepare end up with failed plans, which is why a large portion of serial killers fall under the radar for so long before getting caught. I believe Tiffany Burnes falls under both.

While she is known to plan out the murders of her victims, each text she sent me couldn't have been planned out carefully. Given the context of her words and my location when receiving each message, there is no way she could have predicted what to say to me each time.

In an effort to analyze a psychopath's messages, I wrote down the times, dates, and my locations every time she contacted me and tacked them on to my investigation board.

1/7 1st text message – outside of therapy

1/8 2nd text message – leaving cemetery
1/10 3rd text message – at home sleeping

At first, I found it strange that she chose to text me a day before the anniversary of Chloe's death, which was a day short of marking her return after two years. Serial killers usually stick to a pattern, so why wouldn't she choose to wait another day to send me that first text message? Wouldn't the anniversary of my friend's murder be a day of more significance to make a comeback?

Not if Tiffany thought a better opportunity to scare me presented itself before then such as the moment I left group therapy. The first text conveniently was sent minutes after my therapy session ended; to remind me she's still on the run. What a perfect moment to make me feel guilty about Chloe's death after dishing out my feelings for an hour. The only way she could have found me outside of therapy that day was by seeing me go there before then, by staking me out. The same as I do for a living, Tiffany does for malicious intent. The last time I attended a session was two weeks prior to that day she first texted me. So I surmise she made her return well before then, and had been watching me for a while.

At the time, I wasn't aware of how close in proximity she was to me until I received her second text the next day at the cemetery in Avery. What another perfect moment to guilt trip me even more.

The third text was sent two days later, after I found Cameron—a prime moment to implicate that my client wasn't safe after I rescued him. To make me feel like I put someone else in danger, just as I did with

Chloe. To prove it, she had to take it a step further and show me that she can get close to my clients whenever she wants.

I can only speculate and attempt to get into Tiffany's deranged mind.

As she promised in her first text thread to me years ago, she would be keeping tabs on me and now she is living up to her words.

Throughout the whole morning, I've been skimming through all the recent recordings on our security footage, but I haven't spotted her lurking around our property. I know she was definitely on the side of my house in the blind spot of the camera though because the toolbox is gone. Nobody else would take it and why would they want to, anyways? And how did she know that side is in a blind spot?

I speculate, Tiffany approached my property and saw the toolbox. She wanted another weapon so she grabbed it, thinking the hammer was inside. Finding the steel hole puncher instead was probably a surprise.

If I wanted to sneak onto my property without being seen, how would I do it?

Think like a killer.

As the thought crossed my mind before; the woods seem like a prime place to hide a body…
They are also a great place to hide out if you do not want to be seen.

The only way to watch someone without the other person noticing is from a distance which is what I do for a living. When I stake out my clients in my own investigations, I utilize a camera and binoculars which is how I've solved the investigations that I've conducted.

If I wanted to watch my house from a distance, the only place to watch it from indiscreetly is from the woods.

As long as one person doesn't know the other is looking, they can easily get away with it.

After all, I watched Chloe for months without her realizing and without using binoculars or a camera. I relied on my own eyes and observations back then.

Our outdoor camera that is mounted on our front porch is angled to view our front yard, driveway, and the woods across the dirt road, except it does not have the capabilities to zoom as far as my own camera does.

At my living room window, I test that theory and zoom the lens all the way as far as it allows me to see into the woods across the dirt road. If it weren't raining right now, I would be able to see outside clearly, except all that is in my view is the rain against the windowsill.

"Noah!" I call out as I move to my office to try to look out of my window with my camera too.

Noah and I chose to move to Fairview because we thought living in a desolate area is supposed to be safer. Right now, it sounds like it isn't by my current theory but I believe it still can be.

"I have an idea," I say to Noah when he walks into my office. This time instead of keeping my ideas to myself, I am bringing him along. At this point, nothing that I do or say should surprise him.

"I'm listening." He sits down and leans back in my client's chair.

"As always." I smile. "I am positive Tiffany was here because of the missing toolbox. Like I said, nobody would have stolen it other than her. So, we need to be ready for when she comes back."

"What are you talking about?" Noah shakes his head, sighing.

"We have an advantage on her in our own home. We know this place better than her. As long as we know when she's coming back and we know she will because let's be realistic, an alarm is not going to deter her; we can be prepared for her next time."

"And how are we going to do that? Home alone trap her?" He sighs.

"Well, that's not what I was thinking but if you want to put it like that, then sure. Let's home alone trap her."

4 0

January 15th
2:00 p.m.

Whenever a person enters onto my property, my front door camera, and the camera above the living room window see them. Another camera is set up on the side of my house where the kitchen window is. It is angled toward the road so we can see when somebody drives in. The only way to avoid getting caught on our camera system is by coming from the woods on the other side of the house, where mine and Noah's offices are; the same area of the blind spot on the camera where I was last night.

Now that the rain has finally let up, we came outside to explore the area outside of our office windows for more hidden spots that we might have overlooked. I did not see Tiffany scurrying through the woods through my binoculars and camera from inside my house earlier, but I can't rule out the possibility that she was out there when our alarm woke us up this morning.

The camera app is open on my phone. I watch ourselves walk out of the front door as we head to the left of our house. We keep our backs against the wall, just like an intruder and Tiffany would most likely do.

As we get ready to round the corner toward the backyard, we remain in the view of the camera that is mounted above the front porch. The wet bushes that I planted along the wall to cover the crawlspace of our house, scrapes my ankles within each step. The annoying itch on my skin makes me regret my decision to make this place look homier when we first moved in.

Once we reach the side of the house, we immediately appear on the camera that is set up above Noah's office window. We pass my office, then approach his, which is only a few feet next to mine. We installed the camera here because his window is closest to where the fence starts to block off our backyard. We thought this spot would be the best angle to view everything... but we were wrong. When we step about two feet in front of the camera, I am no longer in the frame.

"Right here. This is where the blind spot begins." I thoroughly inspect the window for any signs of it being tampered with, even though I already made sure the motion sensor inside of the house is still on. Noah attempts to slide the glass open with his left arm while I try to assist him, but it doesn't move. Every time he steps to the left of me, he appears back on the screen. But as long as I remain standing a few feet in front and under the camera where the latch of the window is, I stay out of view.

"Walk to the tree where I said I left the toolbox, but stay close to the wall and fence until you get there," I tell Noah as I enlarge the view from this camera on my phone.

He walks under it, then alongside the permitter of the fence until he gets to the woods. He takes about ten steps past the trees and never appears on camera, so I tell him to turn back around. On his way back toward me, he walks the same path alongside the fence to get to the house.

This would be the perfect way to break-in my home, except it can't be through this window without the motion sensor going off.

"I'll be right back. I'm going to open the window from the inside of the house to make sure the sensor is still working." I know it's turned to the *on* position, but I didn't actually open any of the windows earlier when I checked them. I leave the side of the house and rush around the corner to the front door.

In Noah's office, there is a three-foot tall bookcase in front of his window. There is about two feet of space in between itself and the wall. I lean over the bookcase to unlock and slide the window open. As soon as the glass slides off the track, away from the lock, the sensor immediately blares. I quickly switch it to the *off* position and stop it from ringing.

Out of all the rooms inside of my house, this office is the least used. Besides checking in here for an intruder after the alarm went off this morning, and yesterday when we got back home from checking on Ben and Cameron, I don't think Noah has stepped foot in here in at least a week or so. He uses this place more like storage than a working office.

"When was the last time you were in here?" I ask him through the window.

"About a week ago. I grabbed a file before a meeting," he answers.

"A week ago… when Tiffany started texting me again. How coincidental…" I look around the room, then tell him to come back in here before sliding the window closed, locking it, and flipping the tiny switch on the sensor back to the *on* position. That was not the same alarm sound that woke us up this morning which means the house security system did.

"What are you doing?" Noah stands in the doorway as he sees me gazing around the room, stumped.

"Something tripped the alarm from within this room somehow. It wasn't the window sensors. Besides opening the door after the alarm is set, what else would make the security system on the house go off?"

"The only thing I can think of would be if someone unplugged the wires to the cameras or the alarm system from each other, and plugged them back in." Noah looks at the wires on the bottom of the wall that connect to the camera in our hallway. "You know how all the cameras connect to each other by those wires? Well, when you unplug them, the two cameras that are connected to each other obviously stop working, but when they get plugged back in, the cameras start right back up again. So technically if that happened, then we wouldn't have noticed if we only lost a few seconds of footage. You were fast-forwarding through the footage of last night, so you wouldn't have noticed if the cameras went down for a few seconds."

I direct my attention from the wall to the window. Noah pinned the wire that connects to the camera outside of his window through the screen and, alongside the wall in his office. That camera connects to the one in the hallway by the wires behind the bookcase.

Noah walks over to the three-foot-tall bookcase and begins sliding it away from the window. "Let's test it out and see."

Once the bookcase is out of the way, I am ready to bend down to pull out the wires from each other, but I'm distracted by the floor instead. "What the—"

The wires to the camera are still connected and intact, but the ventilation grate on the floor is wide open.

The cover is unscrewed and left lying right next to the wires against the wall, leaving a hole in the floor to where an air duct should be— a hole leading straight into the crawlspace underneath our house.

4 1

January 15th
3:00 p.m.

The air duct which is supposed to connect to this ventilation grate under Noah's office has been hastily cut away, revealing an opening to the crawlspace beneath the floorboards. With my flashlight shining off my phone, I drop my head down into the hole and hold my breath to avoid inhaling so much dust. It's a tight squeeze to fit my body through, but I am sure it's not for Tiffany, who is skinnier than me. Easily, she can shimmy her way through this quickly. As for her height though, this two and a half to three-foot-tall space has to be a challenge for her.

Tiffany must have accidentally pulled out the wires from each other near the window when breaking her way through the floor last night. The alarm went off and scared her, so she probably plugged the wires back in, and scurried her way back out of the crawlspace through this hole.

The entire crawlspace is not in my direct line of eyesight from here, but I see footprints in the dirt right below me. She was here recently… or still is. I need to get down there and see if she's hiding somewhere around the corner.

But first, I need to find out how she got in from outside. The only way to get down there is through one of the ventilation screens, and there is one in between Noah's window and the fence to the backyard—right behind the camera's line of view.

I shimmy my body out of the hole to get back inside of his office.

Outside, when we approach the bushes on the side of the house near Noah's window, I notice some of the hedging that I planted looks out of shape. The shrubbery looks like it was pressed down or stomped on, then poorly plumped back to place. Just barely noticeable if you're not paying close attention.

We haven't checked this crawlspace or any of the screens that access it since we moved in, and honestly, it wasn't in the forefront of my mind since I planted the bushes around the exterior of the house. The house that we had in Avery did not have a crawlspace, so we never needed to deal with one before.

We push the poorly out of shape bushes out of the way. The ventilation screen to keep insects and animals from going inside, is supposed to be screwed onto the house but it's laying on the ground.

I take my binoculars that are hanging around my neck and peer out into the woods around us. Now that the rain has stopped completely, I fear Tiffany could be out here watching us. That is, if she isn't in my crawlspace instead.

"Ready?" Noah asks as he gets ready to shine the flashlight at the hole.

Nodding, I bend down and begin crawling through on my stomach while holding my gun near my chest. Noah is only able to fit through the hole up to his shoulders, so he aims the light into the space from behind me. In the ray of the flashlight, something a few inches away slightly startles me until I realize it's my pink toolbox. It was blocked by a structural beam when I was looking through the hole from inside of the house, so I didn't see it until now.

All the tools that came inside of the toolbox are still here, except for the hammer, which is still in my office drawer, and the steel hole puncher is gone too.

The light inside of Noah's office shines through the open grate hole. The nuts and bolts which keep the cover intact are in the dirt just below it. A purple screw extraction tool set lays on the ground nearby. That extraction set didn't come out of my toolbox, but I did see the same set of extraction tools in the product details under the purple toolbox on the shop's website.

"Keep scanning the area with the flashlight," I whisper to Noah who is only able to shine it from side to side. I keep crawling the perimeter beneath our home, maneuvering around a few dark corners and structural beams. There is a forty-foot-long hallway around the corner from here where our bathroom and bedroom are above us. Since Noah's flashlight can't help me with this distance, I pull out my cell phone's flashlight.

The further I crawl, I do not see any other footprints or tracks in the dirt other than the ones I'm making. I make my way back over toward Noah's office. This is the only grate that is open with a torn and cut-up air duct.

Out of all the rooms available, why choose this one to break in through? How did she know it was his office? Or does she not know what this room is, and chose a random vent to venture through?

With my phone, I take numerous pictures and videos of the toolbox and its tools, the nuts and bolts in the dirt, and the ventilation hole.

Before leaving, I make sure to cover my footprints and tracks in the dirt while leaving the nuts, bolts, toolbox and its contents left in the same place, untouched. Tiffany will never know I was down here. This is perfect.

4 2

TIFFANY

The past few years that I spent waiting to get back at Ellie are beginning to pay off and my plan is finally about to come to fruition.

Since Ellie stalked me, invaded my personal privacy, and caused me to flee my home in Avery, it was only right that I do the same thing to her. I just never imagined that sneaking around underneath her house would be the only way to do it. Nor did I think it would take this long to execute my revenge. But as much as I have enjoyed tormenting the nosey bitch, I cannot proceed with my fun any longer.

Because of Ellie's impulsive decision to move out of Avery, my plan to kill her got set back. Ellie's antics had proven a challenge for me, but I kept my hopes up and patiently waited until I found her again. And six months ago, I finally figured out her new address.

Then learning she became a private investigator only a couple of months ago was the icing on the cake. Her career change is obviously something she should thank me for, but I won't hold her to it. There was no address for a business under her website where she so kindly boasts about me, but only her email, and new phone number which is what I needed. Then her public voting registration online gave me the most important detail about her; her new address in Fairview.

The short distance between Fairview and Avery made it clear to me that Ellie did not take my threats as seriously as I expected. I scared her enough to move, but not far enough away to feel like I wouldn't come back and find her again. Doubting my capabilities fueled my rage even more.

Did she not realize moving only an hour away made it easier for me to get to her? I lived in Avery for about two years before she took my life away from me and before that, I lived in Jonesville for three. I became familiar with all these towns after all, so hiding out in them comes easily to me. Guess nosey Ellie doesn't know as much about me as she thinks she does.

But I know all about her. I even knew how to break-into her old house in Avery, but upon arriving to her new house in Fairview, I was met with the challenge of an upgraded five-camera setup. Now it became more difficult for me to sneak around without Ellie's observant and obsessive ass seeing me. But even though a bigger camera setup covers more of her new house, that doesn't mean it covers the *entire* outside area.

When you are smart enough to pay attention to the position of a security camera and understand the reason for its placement like I do, it's easy to decipher what the camera is not seeing.

During the years I spent robbing men, I learned how to stake out all the security cameras in the bars and clubs. I could not be seen walking out of a place with a guy I planned to steal from later on in the night. What if the man wanted to find me after I stole from him and went back to the place of where we met? What if he were smart enough to call the police and they'd search through the security footage and find me? There had to be no traces of me with him. I had to think for myself, be a step ahead.

The only way to survive life is to control your environment and that's what I have always done, even before my mother died. Nobody ever looked out for me besides me and that will never change.

It was a hike, but I mapped my way from the main road, through the woods, and over to the side of Ellie's house without being seen. Over the last few months of watching her house and painfully camping out in the woods (something I never saw myself doing, but once again, I can thank Ellie for a new experience that I conquered successfully) I figured out how to get into her house.

One camera is set up above the front door. It seems to be angled to overlook the front yard, driveway, and dirt road.

There is another camera that is set up outside of the living room window that looks like it views the same area, probably just more of the front yard.

A third camera is set up on the side of the house on her kitchen window. It's pointed toward the dirt road.

A fourth camera oversees the backyard which is protected by a six-foot wooden fence that blocks off the woods behind it — the woods where you can't see a person coming from.

And the final camera is attached to the spare bedroom window which is Noah's office, near the fence that divides the backyard.

Out of all the camera angles, the side of the house where Noah and Ellie's offices are, is the least overlooked. The window beneath the camera would be the only way to sneak-in as long as I stayed right under it. But when I couldn't slide it open, the floorplan of the house, courtesy of google, gave me a better option. I examined the layout from the listing that was posted before Ellie and Noah took it off the market.

Sneaking through a window or going through the front and back door wasn't a valid option for me, but one of the ventilation screens to get into the crawlspace would be. What better way to invade her personal space like she did mine, than by invading her home from inside?

Conveniently for me, one of the screens from the outside to the crawlspace is tucked between Noah's window and fence— right behind the camera's view.

The air ducts were the only thing that would be in my way. If I didn't choose to go through the grate, then my only other options would have been to hammer and drill my way through a concrete wall. Then the element of surprising Ellie would be gone.

Cutting away at an air duct wouldn't be nearly as noisy though, and I had plenty of tools to get the job done. Things always come back in full circle. My toolbox not only sufficed as a murder weapon for all these years but the skills I acquired in woodworking class in high school helped me figure out my way to Ellie.

Other than the crawlspace access, the floorplan also told me the house had two spare bedrooms, therefore my hopes relied on breaking into the room that was rarely in use. I know Ellie and Noah do not have kids, and they don't ever have family visitors. So, I figured one of those spare rooms would be designated as an office and last week, I determined I was right. I heard a vehicle pull up to the house, which was immediately alerting because Ellie and Noah were both still home. Then I heard Ellie invite Ben inside, and realized he was an actual client of hers.

I followed their voices to a spare bedroom, concluding it was her office. I had only snuck in the crawlspace four times before that day and each time was in the middle of the night. So, I wasn't sure which spare bedroom was more in use until Ben arrived, and I listened in on his sad attempt to locate Cameron.

Then days later, I came back to spy on her again. The thunderstorm ended up keeping me hostage in the dirt for longer than intended when I did, but now I am thankful for the rain, because all that time I spent down there allowed me to realize the second spare bedroom was the safest way to break-in.

There was never any movement or sound coming above in that room. Then I heard Ellie complaining about Noah's work binder being left on the kitchen table. To which he responded, "What's the sense in keeping it in my office if I don't even work in there?"

And I quickly realized, the only room left for his unattended office was that second spare bedroom.

I couldn't keep coming back in the middle of the night because Ellie is a night owl, so I came back during the daytime. Since Noah works in the backyard, he never heard me sneaking around in the dirt. He never saw me coming from the woods on the side of the house either because of the fence. The few times I bravely crouched and crawled my way beneath the house when he was out in the backyard were reckless, yet I needed to do what needed to get done. I had to sneak-in whenever I had the chance particularly when Ellie was gone, which was only a few chances. I also had a few opportunities to kill Noah especially after he broke his arm, but having a grieving Ellie at home all the time wouldn't have been beneficial to my plan. Seeing her live her daily life in fear felt even better.

I easily cut the airduct in Noah's office off a few days ago when I tricked Ellie into leaving in the middle of the night but I didn't have time to get the cover to the ventilation grate open.

It wasn't until yesterday when I came back to extract the nuts and bolts out of the cover and removed the whole thing. But when I attempted to fit through the hole, a fucking bookcase ended up being in my face. While I tried to push it out of the way, I accidentally pulled out the wire to the camera outside of his window. I plugged the wire back in immediately, but the stupid fucking alarm kept going. By the time I heard it reset itself and turn off, I was already leaving through the vent to the crawlspace outside.

Had I not made any noise after removing the grate cover, both Ellie and Noah would be dead already. If only they knew how much they can thank me for.

4 3

When you push a person to their limits, at one point they break which is exactly what Tiffany wants out of me. Well, I want the same out of her and I can finally say, I am one step ahead of the psychopath who wants me dead.

After I inspected the crawlspace, Noah and I went back to test our original theory about the wires. Now that we know where Tiffany came in from, we still needed to understand how the alarm went off. Turns out, Noah's suggestion was the answer. The connection between the wire from the outdoor camera to the one that runs to the hallway is right above the ventilation grate along the wall behind the bookcase. We unplugged them and the alarm went off immediately. A few seconds after they were plugged back together, the alarm stopped. We assume, Tiffany accidentally unplugged them when removing the grate cover or in an attempt to move the bookcase.

Whatever happened was a mistake of hers and

that tells me her patience to kill me is starting to wear thin.

Since we know how she is coming in through our house, we set up a phone in Noah's office. We do not have any more house cameras from the security system we bought, but a phone works just as well.

I set up an old phone behind a stack of files on Noah's desk and disguised it by a plant. I downloaded a free security camera app that allows me to live stream from any camera device with Wi-Fi. The phone is connected to a portable charger that is also disguised carefully, so it will remain charged until the battery pack itself dies.

The live feed that is coming from the phone in his office is open on my computer and through the security app on my phone as well. We couldn't angle the security camera above Noah's office any further down, or else Tiffany might notice. However, this time we turned the audio setting on, so now we should hear whenever there's movement outside.

I've also been shifting through our footage from last night to see if I can spot when the camera outside and in the hallway went out. I would sit here all day in the dark if my husband didn't pry me away with food right now.

"Can I please turn on the light?" He asks as he walks into my office.

"No. You can see a light on inside if a building from the outside when its nighttime. She can't know we're awake."

"Ellie, if she's coming back here, I doubt it will be anytime soon in this rain." He places a sandwich on my desk, just as lightning illuminates my window. The storm started half an hour ago and hasn't let up. "You need to eat. All you've had was coffee today," he says.

"We should never doubt anything when it comes to that bitch," I mutter while accepting the food.

"Ellie, I'm confident you know what you're doing but I have to admit, this is a little crazy. Are you sure you don't want to call Detective Carner or the police? This isn't safe. I was kidding when I said we should home alone trap her."

"I know you were." I sip my coffee. "Please just trust me. We can't scare her away with the police again. It's too late to tell them anything now anyways. Our plan is going to work."

"You mean, *your plan?*" Noah's sighing and about to protest when we hear a noise coming from my computer but I don't see anything.

"Shh!" I quickly move back over to the window to peer behind the blinds. But I don't see Tiffany outside anywhere.

Noah and I exchange silent glances as we carefully walk into the hallway to listen outside of his office door. Again, we hear something but the sound is so faint, it's hard to identify what it could be.

"Let's go," I whisper and we cautiously, careful not to make noise as we walk across the hall, then into our bedroom.

On my phone, Noah keeps his focus on watching the view from the phone that is set up in his office. He also opens the security camera app from the rest of the house on his phone. Now we can see what her exact movements will be next. I go to grab my gun from the nightstand and turn off the lamp in the bedroom, and close the door. Tiffany expects us to be sitting ducks sleeping, so we must play the part.

I place myself in the far corner of the room behind the door, so that I am not directly in front when it opens. In this moment, my husband could be right. My crazy idea is just that…it's crazy and unsafe. But even though, I agree his worries are valid, my strategy is still thoroughly thought out. I know how Tiffany is getting into my home and I know what she plans to do. I just have to be confidently ready for her, and since we found the open ventilation grate in his office, I can say I am.

If I were Tiffany and I were sneaking into Noah's office, the next room I'd plan to sneak into would be our bedroom— where she expects us to be sleeping, unprepared for her return.

I understand Noah's concern regarding our safety. However, the risk is going to outweigh the cost. It has to.

When only a few minutes pass by, we see the bookcase start to wobble slightly before slowly sliding forward.

The agonizing wait of the return of Tiffany Burnes is finally here, and I'm ready.

4 4

January 16th
3:25 a.m.

In soaking wet and mud filled dirty blue jeans, a black long sleeve and muddy white sneakers; Tiffany Burnes emerges behind the bookcase in my husband's office with makeup running down her face. I expected to see her standing there. However, my reaction still unpredicts me.

Tiffany looks completely different from the woman who I was first introduced to as 'Theresa' in the Go-Go bar back in Avery.

We watch Tiffany fix the crooked black wig back in place on her head through the camera phone. She dusts off her jeans and then kneels down to reach behind the bookcase. As she does, I spot something that is sticking out of her back pocket. Her quick movements make it hard to see whatever the object is though. When she stands back up from behind the bookcase, she holds the purple mallet hammer, which is the same brand of the one that is still sitting in my office drawer. She looks around the room defiantly.

In this moment, I wonder if I made a mistake, leaving the phone on Noah's desk. What if she starts sifting through his things and finds it? What will I do then? But the doubt in my actions surpass me quickly as she bypasses the desk, and heads straight to the door.

When she walked by the phone on his desk, I caught a glimpse of her back pocket and saw the steel hole puncher that I bought. The hallway camera catches the moment the door slightly becomes ajar. Tiffany cautiously pokes her head into the hallway to look toward the kitchen and living room, then to the bathroom in the opposite direction.

Through the camera view in his office, we see her reach into her back pocket for the hole puncher before stepping out of the room.

In the hallway, she holds the hammer in one hand, and the hole puncher in the other. She looks directly at our bedroom door, then begins walking straight toward it.

I bring my attention away from my phone and draw my gun with my right arm toward the door. Resting my left forcarm beneath it, I hold a flashlight in my left hand, and point it in the same direction, but I don't turn it on yet.

Noah stands to the left of me. His role is to keep his cycsight on the phones, while pointing another flashlight toward the door. If his arm was not broken, I would prefer he had his gun pointed at her instead because two guns are better in a fight than one, but with his nondominant hand, it's not.

Besides this fight is between me and Tiffany anyways. I can also take comfort in knowing her weapons are less lethal than mine. I'm the one who brought her into our life. It is my responsibility to take her out.

The doorknob starts to turn and Noah locks his phone. The light of the screen disappears.

We're in total darkness — exactly what this bitch is expecting to walk into.

But the door hasn't opened yet.

Why? What is she doing? Does she know I figured her out? Did I not cover the dirt well after crawling through it yesterday? Does she know that I'm standing in a corner, waiting for her?

Seconds of an eternity pass as Noah and I hold our breaths.

Why isn't the door opening yet? Did I make a mistake? Did I just put us in danger? What if she has a gun after all?

I know she has the hole puncher and the hammer… but what if she's carrying a small hand gun in her bra or waistband that I couldn't see?

I've said it before, I shouldn't put anything past this psycho…

Just as I am rethinking everything, the bedroom door slightly opens. She slides her body through the doorway. She steps toward the bed and I shine my flashlight right at her back and Noah does the same with his. "STAY WHERE YOU ARE!" I shout.

In the light, Tiffany turns around to face us, and steps back, blocking her eyes with her arms; the weapons are in front of her face.

"DON'T MOVE!" I shout again, but even though both mine and Noah's flashlights are blinding her vision, the steel hole puncher flies out of her hand and in our direction. I fire my gun twice. Noah ducks to the ground to avoid getting hit in the head with the puncher as I fire another round.

The steel bounces off my left shoulder, making me drop the flashlight out of my left hand. I gain my footing and fire two more shots blindly in her direction, just as Noah gets up to shine his flashlight again. I am about to fire another round until I realize I am about to shoot at nothing.

"Where the hell did she just go?" I frantically whisper to Noah while he looks at his phone in bewilderment. "I think she ran to the bathroom. The door is closed and we didn't leave it that way."

"Why would she go in there?" I bend down to pick up my flashlight before heading toward the hallway. Does she know that she just cornered herself into a sixty square foot sized room with no way out? She somehow knows the layout of my house because she knew how to come in from beneath it, so why choose the bathroom to corner herself in?

"Wait!" Noah rushes to the nightstand on his side of the bed, opens the drawer, and retrieves his gun to follow me.

As we approach the bathroom door in the hallway, I begin realizing why she made the decision to run in there. The front door is too risky of a distance to run away from my bedroom. Running back through the way she came in from wouldn't have been a smart move either. That escape isn't quick enough to get away and dropping back through the small hole would be a irrational decision anyways, since she knows we know about it. My office door was closed, so she bypassed it and ran straight through the only open door in the house which was the bathroom. She must've thought she could get out quickly through the window through there.

Noah is about to open the door, but I shake my head and tell him to move before shooting once at the door.

I don't hear any screaming or shouting in pain as a response. There is no noise coming from the bathroom at all.

I have six shots left, so I need to make them count. Noah touches my shoulder, gesturing for me to wait and before I can oblige to what he's about to do, he kicks in the door and steps out of my way in the hall.

Immediately, I walk through the doorway and shine my flashlight straight ahead with my gun aimed at the bathtub. The shower curtain is completely shut, but it shouldn't be. Noah and I never close the curtain as a safety precaution. It sounds cliché, checking your bathtub to make sure nobody is in there, but it's cliché because it's true. If you keep the curtain open, no one can hide behind it. Tiffany hid out behind Chloe's curtain before murdering her. So then we shouldn't put it past her to want to do it again.

As I step forward, ready to slide the curtain away, the thought occurs to me; Chloe did not have a gun trained on Tiffany the night she was murdered, so why would Tiffany hide out in my own bathr—

A loud thud and a gunshot only seconds apart from each other echo the small space, causing me to duck out of reflex, and turn around toward the sound.

Then I see my husband laying on his side on the

floor in the doorway. Tiffany stumbles over his body to pick up his gun, which has somehow landed out of the bathroom and into the hallway.

But I regain composure and shoot twice at her back, forcing her to give up attempting retrieval of his gun. She continues running down the hall. I fire again just as she ducks into Noah's office, slamming the door behind her.

I have three more shots left. I rush down the hall, then take a step back for a second to gain distance in case she is ready to lunge at me from the other side. I open the door and in the ray of my flashlight, I see the book case toppled over on the floor, but Tiffany is nowhere in sight.

She will hear my footsteps above the floorboards if I run out of the front door to catch her around the side of the house, and then it really will be a cat and mouse game. That will give her a chance to come back through this grate and get inside of the house again before I can.

I need to make a decision.

Quickly, I rush over to the hole near the fallen bookcase. I drop myself through with my head first. I land on my elbows, and I shimmy the rest of my body down into the dirt. I shine the flashlight toward the outside ventilation screen of where she came through, and catch a glimpse of her dirty white sneakers scurrying out of it.

In this small space, I pull the trigger three more times until the slide on my gun pulls back in a lock position, telling me I'm out of ammo.

I am also incredibly dizzy and my shoulder is throbbing from getting smacked by the hole puncher.

Through the pain, I crawl toward the hole where Tiffany's feet were just hanging out of but are no longer in sight anymore.

Bright spots appear in my eyes… Like the sun is blocking my vision, but I'm not outside yet.

I pull myself out of the hole, then crawl over the bloody hedges, and land on Tiffany's body. She is laying on her stomach, blood running down her back.

I force myself to roll off of her. The pain is becoming unbearable as I stand up. But then my legs give out and suddenly, a sharp pain runs through my left arm and I collapse onto my knees. *But no, I need to stand up and get back to Noah.*

Struggling to regain my footing, I grab hold of where the pain is… and feel something wet…

Fuck. There's blood all over my hand.

SIX MONTHS LATER

4 5

July 16th
4:00 p.m.

Investigators recently confirmed that Tiffany Burnes is responsible for the murder of Jesse Jameson, who was found assaulted to death in a Motel 8 just last week in Brookesview, Florida.

The article from Avery's local news station reporting on Jameson's death is the first story in the list of results when I search *'Tiffany Burnes'* online. Although Tiffany didn't confess to his murder, the autopsy report on his body came back with evidence of the same heart indentation through his skull, as did with her previous victims.

Beneath that article, there's a link to my interview with Fairview's news station which made national television.

Had I never told the internet about my involvement in the Tiffany Burnes case in the first place, I would not have been met with the responsibility to continue filling the public in. With the exception of telling the reporter that my investigation started out with watching Chloe and falsely accusing her of murder years ago, I included every other grave detail.

Instead of including Chloe's name in my interview, I told the reporter that I investigated Tiffany who was introduced to me as Theresa in the Go-Go bar in Avery on my own. Eventually, I presented my evidence to the police department and that's how the Detective began the investigation. Again, I told a version of the truth.

As my concern still stands, admitting to obsessively watching my neighbor, deeming her a killer, breaking into an actual killer's home, and conducting the whole investigation without telling the police first would do no good for my business.

To my surprise though, I've had a slew of new clients reach out to me since my fifteen minutes of fame. Some have reached out in Fairview, while others have reached out from other parts of Florida too.

As I am parking my truck, my phone rings. It's Noah.

"Our telepathy's kicking in," I answer. "I just got here."

"I figured," he says. "I was getting worried."

"I just parked. I'm about to go in now." I turn off the ignition, and take my ID out of my purse.

"Are you nervous?"

"A bit, but I can handle this. Don't worry about me."

"Yeah, don't worry about my wife. Like it's that easy." He chuckles. "I'm proud of you though. I hope you know that."

"I know, but I'm not too proud of how I handled things. I shouldn't have put us through all that. I'm just glad you're alive," I say.

"Well, you're the one who got shot."

"And you got struck over the head with a hammer," I respond and we both bust out into a pained laugh.

"At least the hammer didn't actually kill me like her other victims."

My optimistic husband, always looking on the brighter side of things.

"I know my plan was insane—"

"No, it was not." Noah interrupts me. "The plan was risky, but you did exactly what you thought was the proper thing to do. If we called the police before you made your decision, Tiffany wouldn't be on death row right now. She'd still be tormenting you and killing who knows how many more people."

When the gunshot went off in the bathroom, Tiffany was hiding behind the door; a spot that I should have focused on before coming to the realization she wasn't behind the shower curtain. She slammed the door on Noah's broken arm as she attempted to grab his gun. Amidst their altercation, Tiffany pulled the trigger and the bullet struck my left shoulder before she knocked him unconscious with her hammer. I didn't realize that I got shot because of the amount of adrenaline that was running through me until I was getting out of the crawlspace. I also thought the pain that I was feeling in my shoulder came from getting hit with the hole puncher at the time.

I wanted Tiffany Burnes dead and my full intention was to kill her that night. Except out of the twelve rounds that I shot, only one struck her back and ended up paralyzing her. I thought I would never feel at ease as long as the psycho is alive, but knowing she is paralyzed to a wheelchair in prison with a death sentence is better than her being on the run.

"I'll call you when I leave. I'm going in now. Love you."

"Love you too. Good luck and stay strong. You already outwitted her. You have nothing to fear anymore," Noah says before we end the phone call.

From behind a holding cell where the inmates are transported for one-on-one visits, Tiffany rolls herself toward the bars in a wheelchair. This is the first time I am seeing her true identity; a blond bob, pale skin, deep blue eyes and bags beneath them. What a difference from when I last saw her, unconscious on my lawn.

"Ellie, what a surprise." Tiffany smiles, crossing her arms at her torso.

"Liking your new home?" I look her up and down, then shift my eyes around the cell. "What a fun place to spend the rest of your life."

Tiffany laughs. "Is that why you came here? To try and torment me?" She tilts her head slightly to the left and holds a sly smirk when I don't answer. "Or did you come here to talk about your bestie? You know, some friendships don't always last forever. Although, ours seems to be lasting longer than I expected."

"This isn't about Chloe." I disregard her delusional comment about us being friends and analyze her facial expressions. "I came here to talk about Frederick Garcia"

"Oh? You knew him too?" She remains composed, staring right back at me.

"That was a nice plan you concocted, killing him and taking over his house." I shift my feet. I need to get her to confess to Frederick's murder, so I can get the police department to open an investigation into finding him. If I get Tiffany to admit to what she did, there's a chance we can recover his remains.

"Wow, you really do know me well." Tiffany rolls her chair closer toward the bars of the cell. Now she is only a few inches away. I make an effort not to flinch as she gets closer. This psychotic bitch can't scare me anymore, and I am going to make sure she knows it.

"Frederick was a nice old man, but very gullible, if you ask me." Tiffany rolls her eyes. "And being gullible isn't a good trait in anyone, so I ended up doing him a favor. If I didn't kill him, someone else would have one day."

"Why did you choose him as your first victim?" I raise my eyebrows.

She draws her head back, huffing a grim laugh. "Guess I was wrong when I said you know me well. The first man I killed took place months before I met Frederick."

Good liars know how to manipulate a person well by rehearsing their actions and responses. Tiffany remains still as she is confined to her wheelchair, but the upper half of her body is composed. Her eyes look right at me. No fidgeting hands.

Although it is hard to decipher whether she is telling me the truth about another victim before killing Frederick or not, I can't see why she would be lying.

Why tell me about a different victim when she knows her life of killing has come to an end? There are no chances of her getting out of here and she knows it.

Tiffany rolls even closer to the bars; her foot tapping the metal as she gets closer. I know she wants me to ask about this another supposed victim, but I remain silent and match her stare.

"Did you come here to play a staring game with me too, Ellie?"

"Like I said, I came here to find out about Frederick. How deep into the woods past your backyard, did you bury him?"

Tiffany draws her head back, and smirks. "I'll give you that info in exchange for an apology."

"Excuse me?" I huff.

"I'd like an apology for paralyzing me and putting me here." Tiffany gestures to the small holding cell with her arms out beside her.

"Okay, fine. Sorry for not shooting you in a place on your body that would've killed you instead of only paralyzing you."

Tiffany sighs and begins to turn herself around.

"Wait!" I quickly shout on impulse. There is no way that I am allowing her to get the last word, regardless of whether she'll tell me where Frederick's body is or not.

She stops rolling the wheelchair away, then turns around slowly.

"Okay, you have a deal, but you should apologize to me too," I say.

"For what? Leading you out of a shit job to a more noble one?" She shakes her head.

"You know what to apologize for."

"Oh, you're talking about your dead bestie, Chloe! Sorry that I killed her, but I had to do what I had to do."

"And I'm sorry for doing what I had to do." I look her up and down. Then I smile and mimic her movements, crossing my arms across my torso as well. "Now back to Frederick."

Sighing, Tiffany says, "He's buried about fifty feet past my backyard. Excuse me— my old backyard, thanks to you."

Just as I was expecting. But what happened to the victim before him? If she really killed a different man before Frederick, then that man's body couldn't have been buried in her yard… unless she murdered the both men at the same time. I shouldn't give in, but I need to ask before I leave. "If Frederick wasn't the first guy that you killed, then who was?"

"Nope. Not in our deal." Shaking her head, Tiffany backs her chair away from the bars.

"You might as well give up his name. You're already on death row. Why hold back everything now?"

"I don't know the name." Tiffany shrugs.

"What about where the murder took place?"

"Now why would I tell you that when your job is to find that information out on your own?" She scrunches her forehead, and gives me a mocking smirk in an attempt to belittle me.

"I only spend my time investigating paying clients; people who merit my efforts and are deserving of my services."

"Well then, miss private investigator, to get your

answer, you'll have to come back and ask me another day. My arms ache from all this rolling that you're making me do, and I'd like to lay down now." Tiffany turns the wheelchair around. Her back faces me. Then she looks over her shoulder. "Bye new best friend. I look forward to your next visit."

"I won't be coming back, but I will find out who that man was." I turn around to grab the attention of the guard outside of the door as Tiffany says, "Sure you will. You're obsessed with me."

I face the bar cells, restraining the impulse to grasp them.

"Sure, maybe I was intrigued by you, but I'm also smarter than you and always one step ahead. That's why you're confined to that wheelchair in this hellhole." Tiffany attempts to interject, but I continue on. "I promised that you would get what's coming to you and it is. See you on your date with death row."

ABOUT THE AUTHOR

Sara Kate started her writing career as a scriptwriter for promotional videos and short films. Years later, she wrote her first mystery novel and continues to write full-time in her RV. Aside from writing, she enjoys rollerblading, photography, painting, and anything thriller/mystery related.

ACKNOWLEDGEMENTS

My husband, my father, & special thanks to all the indie authors and readers who support me. To anyone I reached out to in the process of creating this book; to anyone who gave their input in making this story happen, I will forever be grateful.

BOOKS BY SARA KATE

THE WOMAN I BEFRIENDED (Book 1 to THE WOMAN I WANT DEAD) – Several missing men. A suspicious neighbor. A pattern only Ellie sees.

HE THOUGHT I WAS HIS – a stalker thriller (Find a sneak peak of Chapter 1 at the end of this book)

EVERYTHING LED ME TO YOU – a new adult romantic crime mystery/thriller

ZOEY'S MEMORY – a medical mental health mystery

You can find Sara Kate's books on Amazon, Barnes & Noble, Walmart, Target, Books-a-million, and other store retailers! You can also request any of her books to be stocked in your local independent bookstores.

If you enjoyed this book, I'd love to hear your thoughts in a review on Barnes & Noble and Amazon!

HE THOUGHT I WAS HIS

Chapter 1

June 1ˢᵗ

12:22 a.m.

I'm supposed to be the only person in my apartment, but I know my dog did not say bless you to me after I just sneezed.

I get up from my couch in the living room with my bowl of soup when someone knocks on my front door. My dog barks, startling me causing the bowl to fall out of my hands and onto the floor. "Thanks, Lola," I say as I pick her up and carry her to the window beside my door.

It's almost half an hour past midnight and I'm not expecting any company. Then again, I don't expect anyone to knock during the day either.

I don't see anyone in the hallway when looking through the window behind my curtain, but there is a brown paper bag by my doorstep. It's from *Wing Central* which is a restaurant that I often get delivered.

One of my neighbors must have typed the wrong apartment number in an online order though, because I didn't order from there tonight. The delivery person is gone and none of my neighbors are outside, so I guess the food is mine now. Perfect timing, since the knock inadvertently caused me to spill the last of what was in my fridge, anyway.

After setting the bag on my kitchen counter, I pull out three to-go containers; twelve buffalo wings, calamari, and fries. Before eating, I post a photo of my plate on my social media profile with the caption:

Food tastes better when it's free! A black heart and fire emoji.

Minutes later, as I'm eating, Lola barks at another knock and I nearly drop my food again. After six years of having her, I know that she's going to bark every time someone knocks on my door, yet it still startles me.

When peeking through the window behind my curtain, I see a woman walking away from my apartment toward the stairs, so I go outside.

"Excuse me? I didn't order this," I call out to her as I pick up another takeout bag. This one is from *5th Liquors.*

She walks back over to me, looks up at the number next to my door above my mailbox, then back at the receipt on the bag and shrugs. "The address says Apartment 7. It's already paid for."

I bring the bag inside and pull a bottle of wine only halfway out of the bag. It's enough to see the label, *Pinot Noir,* and it's the expensive kind too.

Free food and now free wine in one night? Yeah, somebody must have ordered to the wrong address because nobody would send me this on purpose.

About four hours later, when I am sleeping, Lola abruptly wakes me up by barking. Half-asleep, I sit up and reach over to turn on the lamp that's on top of my nightstand. She's sniffing and scratching the purple carpet under my door. I stumble out of bed, thinking she needs to go out. When I open the door, she immediately races down the hallway, and my eyes follow where she's heading.

She's running straight toward my front door, my front door that's slightly left open, not unlocked but half an inch open.

I *did not* leave it that way before going to bed.

Panicking, I rush over to shut the door and a strong whiff of cologne hits me once I turn the lock. *Did someone just leave or are they still here?*

I turn around to look in my living room and kitchen. Nobody is in either room, but someone could be in the spare bedroom or my bathroom. I ran right past both doors in the hallway once I saw Lola head toward the living room.

I need to call the police and my cellphones in my bedroom, past those two doors. But I need a weapon first. My mace… I need my keys.

Wait, where is my purse?

It's not hanging next to my front door like I normally leave it. My eyes shift to the living room, where I spot my black purse sitting on top of my coffee table instead.

With the mace tightly clasped in my hand now, I head toward the hallway to get to my bedroom. I stop briefly in front of the bathroom on my right. Quickly, I flip the light switch on the wall with one hand while my other hand is still gripping the mace, but no one is inside. *I smell cologne again though.* The back door is still locked. I strung the chain across the top right before I went to bed.

I rush across the hallway and into the spare bedroom. Then I flip on the light switch.

Slight relief sets over me because nobody is here. I only see the bags of clothes that my best friend left me before she moved out a few months ago. The closet doors are still open like normal, and my paintings are on the floor like they should be.

I don't smell any cologne in here either.

I hurry into my bedroom to get my cellphone off the nightstand. When I walk back out, Lola is sniffing every inch of the floor, from the living room to the kitchen. She only does that after somebody, other than myself, has been in my apartment. She sniffs the person's trail of where they walked after they leave. Now she's heading toward the bathroom.

As I frantically call 9-1-1 on my cell, the wine bottle on the kitchen counter catches my eye. *Why is it sitting outside of the bag?* I left it *inside* of the bag, not next to the bag. I remember that because I didn't even pull the wine out all the way.

I examine my apartment while waiting for an operator to answer the phone. Nothing seems to be stolen or out of place.

Except for the wine bottle… and maybe my purse.

THE STALKER

My Brynn's alarm goes off at nine o'clock in the morning. She sets a cup of coffee to brew, then she takes her little useless chihuahua for a walk down to the stop sign. At noon, I follow her to the dog park. An hour later, I see her at the gym. It takes my Brynn about twenty-five minutes to half an hour to complete her workout. I worry about how much cardio she does, but I will talk to her about that when the time is right. At 3:45 p.m. my Brynn heads to work. She comes home about eight to twelve hours later, depending on how busy Moonlit Steakhouse is.

Tonight, she got home at 11:20 p.m. I waited for her to take a shower and get settled in at home before I delivered her dinner. I know she hasn't gone grocery shopping in days, so I decided to order from her favorite restaurant! That's why I brought her so much to eat. I knew she wouldn't eat all of it. I just wanted to make sure that my Brynn has plenty of leftovers until she goes grocery shopping in a couple of days. I don't want her starving. She should not have to result to microwaved soup for dinner.

Ever since her selfish bestie deserted her a few months ago, she's been living paycheck to paycheck, and I do not think it's fair. I am going to change that for my Brynn. Our finances will be my job soon. Technically, they've been my job for a while now. I've been saving for our future for years already. She just doesn't know it yet but when she finds out, she will be so thrilled! And I am going to tell her in a few days, right around her birthday.

I hope my Brynn isn't coming down with a cold because I heard her sneeze when I was outside her door, and she doesn't have allergies. I really wanted to hand deliver the food personally, but no. After I said *bless you*, I panicked. I impulsively spoke out loud when I wasn't ready, left the bag on the floor, knocked one time, then ran like the coward that I used to be. I shouldn't have even been there tonight because being there wasn't a part of my plan.

Sneaking in hours later wasn't a part of it either! I let my impulses take over. I just *had* to see if my Brynn liked her dinner and wine, so I came back to check after she fell asleep. That's something I've never done until last night— sneak-in when she's home. I normally wait to go into her apartment after she leaves, but my curiosity took over because when she only posted a photo of the food on her profile, but not a photo of the wine, I needed to find out why! If she liked the wine, then why wouldn't she post a photo of that too? She liked my choice of food! She posted it! She enjoyed it! I even saw the bones from the wings in her trashcan.

Then Lola's annoying yappy ass got in my way. She barked and I almost dropped the bottle of wine. *Fucking Lola.* That little chihuahua hears everything and I hate chihuahuas. I don't really mind dogs. Personally, I just don't care to have one, especially a chihuahua. I think they are a useless breed of a dog. They do nothing but bark. They don't defend. But I will get past that for my Brynn. I will learn to love Lola only because my Brynn loves that dog like she's her actual child and I would never hurt our children. I admit, before Lola got in my way, I was very disappointed to see that my Brynn didn't open the wine. She didn't even bother to chill it or take the time to admire what an expensive bottle I purchased.

Oh fuck! It was expensive… I'm such an idiot! The wine bottle was too expensive! My Brynn is not used to luxury items. I know this! I overcompensated for my nerves. Shit, I'm glad I didn't stay in front of her door. I would have looked like a jackass with that thing in my hand.

Tonight was a huge mistake. I went off my plan. Her birthday is only a few days away. I must remain patient. For the past four years, I have been waiting. I can wait just a little longer.

To purchase the rest of my books, go to Amazon, Barnes & noble, and Walmart.

www.ingramcontent.com/pod-product-compliance
Lightning Source LLC
Chambersburg PA
CBHW061155210726
48294CB00006B/1687